# the Last Crabtree Girl

# RA ANDERSON

To Mom and Dad for your love, support,
and most of all—the gift of horses.

To my American Saddlebred horse trainers who are no
longer with us but whom I loved so dearly. I wish I could
tell them one more time how much they meant to me.

Mrs. Helen K. Crabtree, Simpsonville, Kentucky

Mr. Charles Crabtree, Simpsonville, Kentucky

Mr. Redd Crabtree, Simpsonville, Kentucky

Mr. Royce Cates, Burbank, California

# PREFACE

Hello, I am Annie. Well, that's what my family called me, but I'm known around the American Saddlebred show arena simply as RuthAnne. This book is based on real stories from a long time ago, created from my personal journals, notes, horse magazines, and memory/photo books that I created from about age ten while living in California. Around age thirteen, we moved to the American Saddlebred Capital of the World in Kentucky. The stories in this book are about when I became a Crabtree Girl at age eleven and rode for Crabtree Farms, Inc., in the heart of Saddlebred country in Simpsonville, Kentucky.

As a young Southern California girl, my life revolved around riding ponies out beyond the mountains to the beaches. I had a deep love and understanding for horses from an early age, spending every day watching trainers work their horses and ours on our family's horse ranch until I was four years old, when Mom allowed me to start riding lessons. Trainers Anne T. Speck and Royce Cates molded me into a little but mighty competitor. To me, showing horses wasn't about winning, but as my father remembers it, my favorite color was blue and that happens to be the color of the first-place ribbon I worked hard to bring home. Riding was my life. The joy of learning, exceeding my personal bests, teamwork, and digging deep within for patience and understanding were all I knew. Riding challenged me! Demanding both mental and physical toughness, wins were an incredible reward for my hard work and dedication. I dared to dream big. At age ten, I left California and traveled to Louisville, Kentucky—with one of my show horses—to show at the World's Championship Horse Show held every year in late summer at the Kentucky State Fair. After that first show, my dream was to compete at the top level. With the support of both my parents, I was able to follow my love of the American Saddlebred horse, chasing my dream of competing in many more horse shows across the United States.

Mrs. Helen K. Crabtree was known as the First Lady of Equitation in the American Saddlebred industry and was a world-renowned horse trainer. As a Crabtree rider, I had the opportunity to achieve my very best through exceptional training and experiences while showing horses all over the United States. Crabtree Farms—which she ran with her husband, Charles, and son, Redd—produced seventy-five World's Champion American Saddlebred horses and twenty-two winners of the National Equitation Championships. Every girl's dream in the Saddlebred industry was to be accepted and trained by such a prestigious player in the industry.

The triumphs I treasured most were mastering riding skills and teaming up with these beautiful, high stepping American Saddlebred horses. Spectacles of beauty and grace, they had their own intense competitor drive. If you ever saw me ride, you would have recognized the joy I was feeling on each and every horse because I was the girl always smiling. Even through some of the hardest rides of my life, I smiled because my heart was full whenever I was on a horse.

My hope in sharing these stories is to inspire you to find what drives you—what is deep inside your person, your heart—and to encourage you to dig deep within yourself to master your inherit skills and keep them polished. Find what you love to do, and don't merely give it your best, but always strive to blow your best out of the water and do better. I cherished the life lessons taught to me as a young girl, riding horses all over the country. I am sharing the lessons taught to me, not only on my horses but important life lessons that I also took away from my experiences. As my horse trainers encouraged me, I, too, want to embolden you to "Go get 'em!" and "Have fun!"

Mrs. Helen K. Crabtree was much more than a horse trainer, wife, mom, and riding instructor. Words simply can't describe her immeasurable love and understanding of animals and humans. Throughout her life, these awards and achievements are only a sample of who she really was:

- First woman to win the United Professional Horsemen's Association (UPHA) Saddle Horse Trainer of the Year

- UPHA Annual Instructor of the Year Award is now called the Helen K. Crabtree award

- She was inducted into the St. Louis Horse Show Hall of Fame and the Illinois College of Sports Hall of Fame.

- Horsewoman of the Year

- Recipient of the AHSA Lifetime Achievement Award

- First recipient of the UPHA Sportsmanship Award

- Winner of the AHSA Lurline P. Roth Good Sportsmanship Award

- Appointed AHSA Judge Emeritus

- USA Equestrian honored her with a bronze trophy to be presented each year to the USA Saddle Seat Medal Finals Champion.

- She designed and developed the Crabtree saddle.

- Helen and Charles were together inducted into the World's Championship Horse Show Hall of Fame.

- She's the author of *Saddle Seat Equitation, Saddle Seat Equitation Revised, Hold Your Horses, Sports Illustrated Book of Gaited Riding*, and she wrote a monthly column for "Saddle & Bridle Magazine" for numerous years throughout her life.


Upon her death, the House of Representatives the General Assembly of the Commonwealth of Kentucky adjourned with a lengthy statement honoring Mrs. Crabtree that included the words, "…she was best known as a riding instructor, and the young women she taught to ride saddle seat were so successful and stylish in the saddle that they were known as 'Crabtree Girls'… When the House of Representatives adjourns this day, it does so in loving memory and honor of Helen K. Crabtree."

The previous quote, spoken by government officials, are now archived in the official Representative Resolutions of the Kentucky General Assembly.

It's been said that she helped make Shelby County, Kentucky the "Saddle Horse Capital" of the United States and "changed the face of the Saddlebred industry."

*Sketch by Helen K. Crabtree 1938-39*

## JOURNAL ENTRY: THE FORUM IN LA, CALIFORNIA

CRISS-CROSS APPLESAUCE, I FOLDED MY legs and held the arms of the stadium chair to keep the seat from swallowing me whole. My gaze was glued on the horse entering the arena as thousands of spectators cheered the last horse and rider. The rider, her eyes on the jump course, made a transition from a trot to a canter, circling before attacking the first jump. It was an easy five-foot jump to help the team build confidence before the next several jumps, where they would be flying over brick walls and triple-bar spreads, combination oxers, and basically a wall of shrubs and flowers, and all averaged almost six feet high. Today, the brick wall was set at six foot, two inches. Future Olympic teams were competing in Los Angeles at The Forum, and my dad was riding with them.

He entered the ring with his horse, Absolutely. As he made the course, the filled stadium seemed to gulp in air at every jump like they did for every team in the competition, but this made it all the more real for me because that's my dad. Dad guided Absolutely around the next corner and prepared for the double bar fence, which was the warm-up into the triple combination. Most everyone cleared this fence; however, it was the fence where speed was everything, and riders pushed their horses to take seconds off their time. One stride more, and they would take off, but Absolutely had something else in mind. He stopped, and Dad flew over the fence, doing a full front flip with a twist and landing on his feet with the reins in his hands, facing Absolutely. Standing at their seats, the audience cheered because they thought it was a spectacular trick. Dad led Absolutely out of the arena because they were disqualified from the competition, but if the audience had had a vote, they would have won by a landslide.

Tonight, the jumps would be set aside, and they would clear the arena for the show horses, along with the American Saddlebreds and Hackney pony-driving classes. Mostly, my mom and her horse trainers show these athletic, high-stepping, elegant creatures. The more excited the horse, the more the crowd cheers them on. And the hairs on my arms always stand straight up while goosebumps run up and down my body. One day, I will be showing. One day, maybe I will be in the Olympics or showing at the World's Championship Horse Show. It's all I dream about, but first, I need to learn how to ride better. I can't wait to go home and practice on Fame.

## JOURNAL ENTRY: MY STURDY STEED

FAME IS A HANDSOME PALOMINO quarter horse of a creamy color with a white mane and tail, and he belongs to my mom. When I entered his corral this morning, his big head—with the big white blaze running down his face—was lowered down to my height. His lips almost touched the ground as he stared at me, then he nudged me gently and almost knocked me down. I snapped the lead line on the lower loop of his halter underneath his jaw, swung open the gate, and led him toward the barn. Between the feed barn and the stall barn, I tied him to the horse hitch. That hitching post reminds me of old western movies where the cowboys ride into town, tie their horses up, and walk into the saloon, but this is where I groom Fame. Grooming has to be done every day before and after I am allowed to ride him.

My groom bucket has a curry, hard brush, soft brush, a hoof pick, a hand towel, and a large comb for his main and tail. When I was done picking his hoofs out and brushing his legs, shoulders, and chest, instead of waiting for someone working at the ranch to finish his top half because I can't reach, I found a small ladder to stand on and worked my way around. He stood patiently, waiting for me. When the brushing was complete, Fame put his head down, allowing me to wipe his face off with the towel and comb his forelock, then I slipped his halter off and put his bridle on. I then walked him into the arena, led him up next to the fence, climbed to the top of the fence rails, and as I reached across his withers at the base of his neck while holding the reins, I grabbed a handful of his mane and jumped. Landing on his back and withers, I pulled myself farther onto his back, swung my leg over, and was set to ride. My most favorite place in the world is on a horse's back!

Riding him around the arena, I watched the trainers work other horses and give lessons to everyone but me. Even my brother, DJ, had a jumping pony named Dudley Do-Right, and I begged to have lessons on him, but everyone said I was too small. Dudley was bay-colored, caramel-brown with a black mane and tail, and he can jump anything in his way. Dad shows the jumpers that go over fences made to look like brick walls, and when he isn't jumping these towering walls, I stand behind them and use them as shade from the hot summer sun. One day, Mom was in a hunter jumping class, and her horse refused a jump. The horse stopped right before the jump, and Mom didn't. She broke her leg and decided she liked showing her American Saddlebred horses better. Dad continued showing his jumpers for a while.

One of my favorite horses at our ranch is Liza's Lady Jane. Liza is a bright red sorrel Thoroughbred mare with kind eyes and really super long legs. She's one of the tall-est horses I've ever seen. My parents tell two stories about me and Liza from when I was really little, maybe around two years old. I only kind of remember, but I really like Liza and could see it happening. These two stories are my favorite, and I love to hear my parents tell them over and over again.

As the story goes, Mom and Dad were standing near a corral where a two-year-old filly named Liza was lying un-der a shade tree. I had toddled into the corral and crawled onto Liza's back. When they noticed, they had to try hard not to panic and frighten Liza because if she stood, I would not only fall and hit the hard dirt, but Liza might step on me. So, they could do only one thing, coach me off the young mare. As they bribed me to come to them, Liza reached her head around and sniffed me. She never tried to stand, allowing me to slide off her safely, and as the story ends, I lived. A couple years later while walk-ing down the barn aisle, Dad noticed Liza's stall door was slightly open. Dad couldn't imagine why the stall door of the then four-year-old Liza would be open or who would be in her stall because the trainers were gone for the day. He looked inside through the bars and saw Liza lying down with me snuggled up between her legs and fast asleep. She was just lying there looking at me, smell-ing my hair, as I rested on her leg as a pillow. Dad says he had no idea what to do but try and wake me without scaring Liza. Again, she could have stood up and crushed my four-year-old self. He managed to wake me up from my nap, and once again, Liza didn't kill me.

Mom showed Liza for a couple years in the hunter

classes, but after she decided to show more Saddlebred horses, Liza was retired from showing and became a broodmare. Mom has a picture of me sitting on Liza in that same corral, bareback, without even a halter on her, and Liza's foal at her side. We were facing away from the camera, and I was looking back and down at the foal. I've never ridden Liza while training; there is simply something special between her and me.

# CHAPTER 3

T HIS WAS THE DEAL. I had to canter Fame before Mom and Dad would buy me my own pony. I used fences and gates to climb on top of his bare back and walked him around for hours and hours. When I felt ready, we advanced into the next gait, a trot. I was determined to get my own pony, and with months of practice, the better my balance became and the more confidence I gained. Soon after, I cantered him. It wasn't without slipping from side to side on his bare back. I held on with my legs, riding with one hand on my reins and one hand gripping his mane, anticipating his lunge forward into a canter.

A deal is a deal. The challenge has been met. Mom and Dad watched me canter Fame around our large arena and then added to the challenge, saying that I needed to canter both directions, on both leads. They later admitted that they thought they would have at least a year before needing to look for a pony for me. So, while I was mastering cantering Fame both directions of the arena, they were busy searching for a pony. It appears that I love challenges and had no problem rising to this very special occasion.

It was winter when I conquered cantering Fame in both directions of the arena and learned what leads meant. It's like when you skip, the leg that is forward is the leading leg, but the hard part was remembering which was left and right. My shortcut for learning my left from right is remembering my teachers make me write with my right hand. In the arena, if you track to the left so the rail is on your right, you would need to canter on your left lead. If you are on the correct lead, it balances the horse while making a turn. Racehorses canter down the long sides on their right lead and do a flying lead change to their left lead. This balances themselves in the turns tracking to the left, but it's done so fast, you can hardly tell. At least that's what Mom and Dad's racehorse trainer friend told me.

Vicky and I have been best friends from the day they unloaded her from the trailer. To surprise me, they told me a goat was in there and that I had to come see it because it was so cute. I was there before the trailer stopped because I loved all of our animals, including the box turtle that tried to pinch my finger off. Needless to say, I couldn't wait to see the cute goat. But I froze when a beautiful soral Shetland pony with flaxen mane and tail, which is code for every color a horse can have mixed together, making a grayish brown. She is little, like me, at about fifty-four inches tall. Her forehead has a little white star, and her cute little ears pointed forward as she looked around while walking off the trailer. She is the most amazing thing I have ever seen, and we are best friends. My legs don't go past the bareback pad on her back, but together, we explore the hills and mountains around our ranch—every valley, lima bean, and strawberry field—and we have even snuck through fences and explored the Eucalyptus forest. I've been known to ride all the way to town—4.5 miles one way—just for a candy bar, and of course, the hard jelly candies called Jujubes for Vicky!

# CHAPTER 4



A S DAWN BROKE OVER THE Black Mountains in the east, a rooster crowed. The wind carried a faint call from the young lambs in search of their mothers, who were probably only feet away. Those silly lambs. It seemed Scott, the ranch's caretaker, had already started the morning feeding. Since today is Saturday, his oldest kids, Dawn and Daniel—who are my age—were helping him feed all the animals.

Carefully sliding off my bed so as not to disturb HoneyBear, my calico cat, I put on my jeans, boots, and T-shirt before heading to the barn. Passing the plum tree, I snatched one off the branch and ate the sour fruit for breakfast. It wasn't quite ripe, but the sour reminded me of SweeTARTS. Mornings are my favorite time of day because of the cool air and all the baby animals awake and talking. By the time everyone was fed, Scott had started cleaning the stalls, and the horse trainers arrived to work with the horses. We have had horse trainers here for as long as I can remember. I watched them groom the horses, brushing and rubbing their coats, picking out their hooves, and doctoring scrapes, but I love to watch them ride the horses the most. I sat on Fame and worked with him in the ring, following and copying everything they did. Well, at least I was going in the same direction as they did. When they walked, I walked. When they trotted, I trotted. When they cantered, I cantered. Well, sometimes. As they left to get the third horse, I went to get Vicky. I groomed her, put her bareback pad on, led her to the arena, climbed up one fence rail, and plopped onto her back, pretending to work her. I played "horse show" and watched each trainer give Mom and DJ their lessons. I also watched my dad jump his horses, but I wasn't allowed in the arena when the horses were jumping fences. However, with some begging, Mom and Dad allowed me to show DJ's hunter pony, Dudley, in some rail classes at the small shows. They also trailered Vicky to the smaller horse shows so I could ride her around. Soon, my two best friends had their parents bring their ponies, and we rode around the shows together.

Every day about lunchtime, the trainers went home. After riding Fame and Vicky for about a year, Mom and Dad purchased my first American Saddlebred show horse for me. Her name is Hello Dollie, but I call her Dollie for short. When I first saw her, I thought she was Dudley. They could have been related except for the fact that they are two totally different breeds of horses.

Our horse ranch, Plaza Del Caballo, is in Rancho Santa Fe, California. Mom is the ranch manager, and we have Thoroughbred show jumping horses, Hackney show driving ponies, and American Saddlebred show horses. However, most of the Saddlebred show horses are at a stable near Los Angeles, in Burbank, with Mom's Saddlebred horse trainer, Royce Cates. He lets me call him Royce instead of Mr. Cates, and being located near Hollywood, most of his clients are movie stars and even a Nevada state senator. Well, besides us. Sometimes, he takes us riding through Griffith park when he thinks the horses need to see something other than the riding arena.

Mom looked for an American Saddlebred trainer who could come to our ranch instead of all of our Saddlebred horses being miles away. Some would stay with Royce, and the others could be at home. That's when she found Anne, who started training horses at Plaza Del Caballo when I was about four. I watched her from the time she arrived to the last horse she worked, but most of all, I loved to watch her train and work the horses. At lunchtime, she would go home, have lunch, and work her horses at her own ranch, Rancho Del Mar.

I bet she thought my parents were crazy when they asked her to buy show horses for me when I was only five. Anne taught me everything, from how to hold the reins of a show bridle to actually showing at the horse shows. Show bridles have a snaffle bit, a curb bit and a rein connected to each side, totaling four reins. In order to work the bits correctly, you have to hold them a certain way. It was hard at first, but Anne bought me little skinny reins I could hold better. It allowed me to learn how to feel the contact with each bit and how each bit worked in the horse's mouth. She gave me lessons almost every day. What Anne didn't teach, I watched and learned. I shadowed her whenever I was allowed. Anne prepared me to show Dollie, and I guess you could say Mom groomed me to look the part of a real showman. Before I started riding Dollie, I could picture myself riding in the Olympics, but we switched over to the Saddlebreds, and now my dreams were to become a world's champion.

Mom purchased a riding suit, hat, and boots for DJ and me. Saddlebred riding habits are different than the hunt-seat habits that we wore to show the hunters. Those are like what riders in the Olympics wear. American Saddlebred habits remind me of what businessmen wear, or men's dress suits from the old days when they wore a derby hat, like the hat Mr. Banks wore in Mary Poppins or Stan Laurel wore in the Three Stooges. Dad told me that the felt derby hat was invented by two hat makers from London in the mid-1800s. It was originally called a Bowler because the Bowler brothers invented it to protect riders' heads from low hanging branches. The hat completes the look and style of the riding habit.

My suit jacket, pants, and matching vest are navy blue with thin brown, black, and tan pinstripes. My paddock boots are black, and I have a light blue button-down shirt, a navy pinstripe tie, and a navy derby hat. The jackets are longer than a man's suit, and the coattails drape down the rider's thigh to just above the knees. The pants are referred to as jodhpurs, or jodhs for short. The legs are longer than normal dress pants and fitted so I don't have high-waters when I sit in the saddle. The pant legs are kept in place by straps called tie-downs. I couldn't imagine showing with my pant leg creeping up my leg and bunching up between my saddle and knee. That would hurt! Even though these suits and riding habits sound ridiculous, they work. They are fitting for this style of riding.

I entered my first Saddlebred horse show with Dollie in three-gaited classes and equitation classes. Equitation is judged on the rider and how well the rider makes the horse perform. Three judges oversee the performance classes, while only one of them judges the equitation classes. Anne had to teach me how to do patterns for shows. That's when the judge wants to see how well you can make your horse do things like a figure-eight or two big circles at the end of the arena, either at a trot, a canter or both…whatever the judge asks to see. Anne taught me more than how to ride. She taught me that I am enough just as I am, even if I am as small as a peanut.

# CHAPTER 5

JOURNAL ENTRY: COCONUT & SWEETPEA

My family is so into horses that when Mom, Dad, DJ, and I went on vacation to visit family in Utah, we somehow came back with two beautiful Welsh ponies named Coconut and SweetPea. Coconut is a hunter-type pony with a Thoroughbred physique. Her head and neck are level with her back, and she has a smooth flowing stride, her legs and hooves reaching way out in front of her. She is black with two short white socks and a crooked white blaze. Her eyes are big and dark brown, and she has a peaceful, sweet way about her. SweetPea looks the Saddlebred show type with a high-arching neck. She is a silver dapple gray, with three white socks and a thin white blaze. Her dark blue eyes, almost a midnight gray, show more excitement in them than Coconut's eyes. Anne worked SweetPea like a Saddlebred, and she soon gained strength in her legs and came up level with leg motion. Her hooves come up at least level to her knees. It was quite impressive turning a Welsh pony into a high-stepping show girl.

Anne trained both ponies to pull a cart, and I was so

excited to learn how to drive. The two biggest challenges were that my feet didn't reach the floor of the cart, and the cart without the floor had these stirrup things, but my feet didn't reach those either. And second, I can't see in front of us and have to peek out and off to the side. I would think it's like driving a car with something covering the windshield, so you have to hang your head out the window to see. The next hard part was not to smile. If you do, you get a mouth full of the dirt being kicked up. I had fun, but I would much rather ride than dodge dirt clods.

Mom and Dad take me to weekend shows where they show their hunters. Coconut and I show in several different classes. One of my favorite shows gives huge stuffed animals as trophies. My best friends and I have a lot of fun showing our ponies together. Costume classes are my absolute favorite, and my next favorites are the bareback classes.

At the Saddlebred shows, I ride in combination classes. They are fun! You drive the pony to work both ways of the ring at the commands of the judge. The announcer calls out which gait to perform and when to reverse directions. After the judge finishes, we are asked to line up in the middle of the arena. This is when trainers like Anne bring the saddle, the bridle, and someone else to help, and they switch the tack from the harness and buggy to saddle and bridle. The funniest part is watching Anne run out of the arena pulling the cart like a horse. When the whole class is tacked up and mounted, the same ponies and riders are judged as an under-saddle class. The first year, Tina—an older juvenile rider who also helped Anne at her barn—showed SweetPea, and I showed Coconut. "SweetPea is a bit of a handful," is how Anne put it. I was glad Tina was able to show her, except she always won, but these classes allowed me to watch Tina. I am so envious of how well she can ride. Showing with Tina has not only allowed me to watch my idol ride, but it taught me to be aware of everything in the arena and watch where I am going.

# CHAPTER 6

## JOURNAL ENTRY: LEARNING TO FLY

HORSES LEND US THE WINGS we lack because of the freedom we feel when riding, and sometimes because of the speed they can take us. DJ, my older brother, likes speed. Motorcycles, dirt bikes, BMX races, skateboarding, and fast horses. When Dollie came into my life, so did a little five-gaited pinto named Hercules. Pinto is Spanish for "painted horse," like the horse named Cochise that Michael Landon rode in the TV show, Bonanza. I love that television show. Five-gaited horses do an extra two gaits besides the walk, trot, and canter. They also do a man made gait, but it's apparently in their DNA. One gait is slower than the other, and they are called the slow-gait and rack. They are a four-beat gait, so only one foot is on the ground at a time. It's pretty amazing, and boy, can this little black and white pony move fast.

The rider sits back on their pockets, squeezes with their thighs and calves while pushing down with their heels, and lifts and spreads their hands a little while bumping their reins, slightly touching the horse's bit one side and then the other. I don't know how it's taught to a horse, but it is smooth to sit to, and did I say fast?

DJ has a new chestnut gaited horse named Secret Call, but he is riding Hercules to learn how to rack better. Guess who started to ride Hercules? Yep, I did! It was my first time feeling the excitement of the gait called a rack. "I feel the need for speed." I pictured holding a sword, or jousting while speeding toward my enemies, or racking away from a swarm of killer bumble bees. Dad said General Robert E. Lee's gray horse, Traveller, was an American Saddlebred most notable for speed, strength, and courage. I like to think of the American Saddlebred horse as being agile, elegant, athletic, and fun. Thinking of Hercules always makes me smile. The small but mighty Hercules.

Five-gaited juvenile classes in California are filled with girls and boys ages seventeen and under, but there isn't an age limit for being too young, nor is there a speed limit. At age seven, I sat on top of Hercules in the warm-up area, waiting for the bugle call official announcement for our class to enter the show ring. Six-foot boys on their tall and super elegant horses stared down at little Hercules and me, wondering if we were for real and probably thinking there was no way this little four-foot peanut on her little black and white pony was going in their class. I was awestruck by their horse's beauty but focused my mind on one thing and one thing only—my horse and riding in this class. Dad said Hercules and I were the underdogs of the class, but Hercules has two things in his favor—heart and speed. I was told the more I ask of him, the more he will give me and the better he will show.

When we trotted into the arena, the judge's attention

was on the big fancy horses trotting down the straight-a-way, and they only took a mental note that this little spotted pony with a tiny little girl was there. Rarely did I notice a judge write our back number down, but that never stopped me from trying to change their minds. We were asked to walk, and a moment later, to slow-gait. Hercules and I tried our best to stay at the same speed as all the large, fancy horses, but I was also taught to get ready to pass several horses when we turned the speed up to a rack. Making my way off the rail, I heard the announcer say, "Rack on." Hercules heard the call too, and my legs flapped a little kick up against my saddle as he dug down deep and went as fast as I felt safe. We passed horse after horse. Some horses broke out of gait, and some pinned their ears at us. As we made the next turn, I noticed the crowd cheering, and it seemed to be following me around the arena.

"Walk," I heard the announcer say, and then we cantered. Hercules had a canter that you could only imagine a merry-go-round horse would have, slowly rocking you forward and back. When we reversed directions, the crowd stayed with me even at the trot. I was confident the people's choice award was going to Hercules, but I wondered how I could win over the judges. As we racked our way past more horses, I noticed the judges watching me. I even saw them smile as I smiled while riding past them. The cheering was so loud that I almost didn't hear the announcer call for the walk. After the canter, we lined up as the judges made their way over to us. Stopping at Hercules and me, they said things like "Did you have fun?" and "I didn't expect that today!" and "Good job, you two." They also took my number down while I was in the lineup! I saw them walk back behind me and write my number down. No matter what ribbon I won—sometimes it was blue, but most of the time, it was third or fourth, or even ninth or tenth—I knew I had won the crowd's heart because when I picked my ribbon up from the ringmaster, the crowd went wild. They cheered for Hercules until we were outside of the show arena, thus causing goosebumps to multiply up and down my arms.

I've known Royce my whole life, but I didn't have any horses with him until after I showed Hercules for about a year or so. He is actually who Dad purchased Hercules from. Apparently, Royce had him in training for a boy who ended up being too scared to ride him because he is very fast. Royce thought I could handle a more advanced five-gaited horse and purchased a five-gaited chestnut gelding named Split Second for me. It is so exciting to ride with Royce as my trainer. He seems bigger than life to me. Maybe because his customers are movie stars, but I think the real reason is that Royce is more like a grand-father to me but with super training powers. He had to teach me how to show a speeding bullet, and I learned how to grip really hard with my legs because Split Second flies! Royce wasn't a fan of allowing his riders back in the stall area, so I wasn't allowed to visit with Split Second. Each time he was led out for me to ride, while whoever was holding him became preoccupied with tightening his girth or putting my stirrups down, Split Second would lower his head down and sniff me. Our first show season was a real success.

In the "National Horseman" magazine, October

1977 issue, someone wrote, "Phenomenal nine-year-old RuthAnne has invaded the magical world of show horses this season, and she rode her unbelievable Split Second to win the prestigious juvenile five-gaited championship at Del Mar. With her top bay walk-trot pony Hello Dollie, RuthAnne was English pleasure Championship at Del Mar, and climaxed the show with the High Point Saddle Seat Championship.  She was honored as the only rider in Del Mar history to win each of the three juvenile championships while riding in the youngest age division."

## JOURNAL ENTRY: COCONUT & VICKY

N THE THIRD GRADE, I started going to a school at the bottom of the mountain from our home and ranch, and by the second month of school, it had become incredibly hard for me to leave my best friends—my ponies—at home. Weekends were filled with adventures on Vicky or Coconut, blazing new trails across the fields and up in the mountains. Coconut is a sweet pony, but give her an excuse to get me off her back and she will. And she's harder to get back on than Vicky, so I had to pay attention to things around us that might scare her because that would be the perfect excuse for her to lunge sideways and leave me on the ground. Besides that, she loved to be around people. Once I even rode her to school. The teachers had everyone come outside and ask me questions like it was a show-and-tell. Everyone loved petting her and feeding her grass. Vicky would have taken a bite out of someone or kicked them if they stood too close to her behind. Vicky is my favorite and always will be, but don't tell Coconut because I love her too. If I need to get off Coconut for any reason, like to open a fence or anything, I have to find something to stand on. This one day at school, I used the playground's ladder to jump back on her. At lunch, I took her back to our ranch and had to walk all the way back to school before lunch break was over. I was late.

Vicky is short enough that I can hop on her without standing on something, but that took a couple of years of practice and growth. Plus, if I don't hop on fast enough, Vicky will turn her head and bite me on the butt. Once she bit me so hard, I couldn't sit down for the whole weekend. I even ate dinner standing up and had black and blue teeth marks to show for it. Even though she makes me cry sometimes, we are the best of friends. I taught Vicky to rear up and take off just like the Lone Ranger does in the television show. We do the "Hi-ho, Silver, away!" move and take off in a blazing gallop to the unknown. When I was first teaching her this trick, she ran me right into a pomegranate tree. Pomegranate trees are like bushes with thin, firm branches, so landing in it felt like I flew into a pile of sticks pointing in my direction. I rode her bareback, and she ran close enough to the tree to toss me into it a couple times. I guess I was a slow learner or trusted her too much. I had scratches all over from that branchy tree, but soon we mastered the "Hi-ho, Silver" move and raced off together. We gallop down the dirt road, her hooves hardly touching the ground like we are flying. DJ rides his motorcycle up next to me and challenges us to a race, and for some reason, I accept, and off we go. DJ's motorcycle quickly leaves Vicky and me in the dust. It is dusty, but it is fun!

I plan on dressing Vicky and I up as witches for Halloween if Mom and Dad will trailer us to a subdivision.

I can't imagine teaching Coconut to race or go trick-or-treating with me, but she enjoys being ridden and loves to explore the farm with me. Coconut and Vicky are complete opposites. I can tell by the way they use their eyes and ears. Vicky's eyes dart around, and she uses her ears last, giving little warning if she is about to kick or bite. Coconut's eyes take everything in but in a more relaxed, easy-going way. This is how I can tell so fast if she's thinking of bolting from underneath me. It's when I am not paying attention that she gets the best of me. Ponies are unpredictable, but that's also the reason they are so much fun. Coconut doesn't like to be too far from the farm. She seems to get nervous, but Vicky loves to explore the trails. I am convinced if a rattlesnake came after us, Vicky would pounce on it and Coconut would take off, but hopefully, we will never find out!

# CHAPTER 8

JOURNAL ENTRY: I'VE GOT HIGH HOPES FOR
THE CALIFORNIA HORSE SHOWS

DJ, MOM, DAD AND I drove into the stable area of the Del Mar racetrack, where everyone stalled their horses for the Del Mar horse show. The show arena was close to the main road, opposite the racetrack. We spotted our barn because of the blue, red, and white stall drapes with the wooden sign for our farm name hanging in the front. A couple of large twenty-by-twenty pictures of Mom showing her horses hung on the outside wall. In front of the stall draped with this heavy polyester covering was a sitting area, holding four folding chairs and two director chairs with Plaza Del Caballo embroidered on the backs. Mum planters lined the sitting area, and against the stall drapes were two brand new wood tack trunks with "PDC" monogrammed on the front sides. Dad let us out and left to go park the car.

On the opposite end of the barn aisle were stall drapes in the same color, but decorated with the words, "Rancho Del Mar." A shield in the shape of a police badge also decorated it, and "RDM" was written diagonally down the middle. In small print on the bottom left were the words, "Rancho Del Mar," and in the upper-right corner was a sketch of a saddle horse. There were chairs and flowers that matched Plaza Del Caballo, making the two horse ranches look like bookends with the stalls in between. Tiger, Anne's Ridgeback dog, was lying outside the tack room, looking as if he was in charge of guarding everything. Mom instructed me to sit in the tall director's chair so she could put my hair up. She put all my light brown curls in a ponytail that sat low, near my neck, then braided it. She then rolled the braid around my ponytail holder and put in hairpins to secure it in place. This isn't my favorite thing because she jabs the hairpins into my head. I am truly surprised I never bleed. This is my least favorite part of a horse show, but getting all dressed up is totally cool. I was completely dressed to show, and the only thing I had left to put on were my black leather riding gloves. Then we sat and listened to the announcements updating the stable area on what class is in the arena and what is going on, like, "Class number forty-eight has reversed directions and working at a trot." Riders get on our horses early enough to warm them up. They are athletes. Dad explained to me that an Olympic runner wouldn't go from their couch into a race, and nor would I want to have a horse get hurt. When the sound of the bugle is heard, which is typically done by the organist making the sounds of a bugle call, the paddock announcer lets everyone know the class is being called into the arena. I guess this is the typical start at any horse show.

Most Saddlebred horse shows on the west coast are in

California, and there are several in Arizona. Each show has an organist who plays throughout the show. I guess it's a horse show thing. A horse name doesn't mean much as an equitation class because the horse's names aren't mentioned. Equitation is judged by 60% rider, 40% horse, and combination of horse and rider. So, the announcer announces the equitation winners like this: "First place goes to number 102" before stating the rider's name. But in a performance class, the announcer says, "First place goes to number 409" before stating the horse's name. I guess that's how all announcements are made.

As I entered the show arena, I heard the organist play, "Hello Dollie." Goose bumps ran over my neck and cheeks, tickling me. Listening to her song made me want to sing, and I smiled extra big the whole class long! We retired Dollie, a tribute to years well done after the end of my U9 (under nine years old) show career.

Mom and Dad purchased a new equitation horse for me, a tall, dark—almost black—handsome, long-necked Saddlebred gelding named High Hopes. His neck is so long I can hardly see in front of us when riding him. I peek between his ears to see the way. I will really miss showing Dollie, but now I've got High Hopes. After riding Dollie and Hercules, High Hopes feels like I am riding a giraffe. His head rises up, and he sets himself right into my hands and face. If I want to lean forward to kiss his neck, I only have to move forward a few inches. The first couple of times I showed him, he raised up so high that I seriously could not see over his head. I learned a new meaning of the phrase that most instructors and trainers say: "Look straight ahead, between your horse's ears." Anne and

Tina smile at me and giggle. They call me Peanut. I just smile and enjoy the attention from my two favorite horse people. The bonus was Tina being there. She was in the older age-group and is the best juvenile rider in California. She most likely can beat any rider on the east coast. Tina showed High Hopes a couple times before I did, to let Anne see what he would do in a class before I showed him. I am the luckiest girl around because I have Anne and Tina helping me with my new equitation horse.

The first time I showed him, I entered the arena, all business and serious about the ride, and what song is coming from the speakers? The organ player was playing Frank Sinatra's song, "High Hopes!" It took all of my power not to sing along with it. Around the arena we went, almost dancing and singing.

Hackney road pony classes are fun to watch. It's amazing how the drivers can see where they are going, where I have trouble seeing around a pony. The jog is one thing, but when the announcer said, "Turn them on," I was completely amazed by the class of speeding ponies. My combination classes are in slow motion compared to these Speedy Gonzales ponies. These are cheering, yelling, crowd pleasing classes. I wondered how they manage not to run each other over. Mom has a little Hackney road pony she shows. I sit near the rail to watch, waiting for her to enter the class and to cheer her on. The class enters the jog tracking to the right, so they enter the opposite direction as the show horses. It's like a warm-up. If you were racing Thoroughbreds or Standardbreds on a race track, they race going to the left. As I sat waiting for Mom to enter her class, I heard the first few measures of the organ play something out of the ordinary. It was the theme from *Batman*! The organist was playing Na, na, na, na, na, na, na, na, na, na, na, na, na, na, na, na, Batman! As Mom entered the arena. Goose bumps ran up and down my arms as she drove him past me, and I cheered. Her road pony's name is Batman!

# CHAPTER 9

## JOURNAL ENTRY: RIDING BY THE SEAT OF MY PANTS

Split Second lives up to his name. He makes it from one end of the arena to the other in a split second. He trots so fast I barely need to post. You can't sit to it, but it's impossible to post that fast. "No guts, no glory," DJ always says. Split Second takes all I have to hold on and ride! I only get to ride him at shows and when we drive all the way up to Burbank to practice, and it's a long drive.

Dad has driven me to Burbank for my lessons with Royce a few times without Mom, and normally, Royce rides Mom's horse, Denmark's Aquarius, so Dad can see his progress. Aquarius is a big, powerful gelding. Royce shows him in the open classes, and Mom shows him in the amateur classes. One day, Royce had his groom help him with the tack after a short ride, and he looked back at me and said, "Do you want to ride him?" Without hesitation, I walked over to Aquarius and waited for a leg up. They had grabbed my saddle off Split Second and tossed it onto Aquarius's back already. He was so fast and powerful, it was like riding a freight train! I don't know if anyone told Mom, but it was one of my most thrilling rides. Royce trusted me, at age ten, enough to put me on this powerhouse of a horse. My heart beat faster and harder than I've ever noticed. I had to think fast and listen carefully. His powerful body tossed me up in the air so high at the trot, it was hard to land on time for the next post upward! His slow gait was too fast, but I wasn't strong enough to hold him up and back. We didn't make a mess of it, but it could have been better. He took my breath away. If all top American Saddlebred horses feel like this, sign me up! Riding Aquarius made me realize that riding Split Second was easier than I thought, but he was still a challenge to keep up with.

## JOURNAL ENTRY: AND THEN I FROZE

STRANGE IS FLYING ACROSS THE country to ride in a horse show, and showing at the biggest horse show of them all seems unreal. Royce is friends with one of the top American Saddlebred trainers in the world, Mr. Tom Moore, who has won so many world's championships, I don't think he could keep up with how many. Mr. Moore agreed to take High Hopes to Louisville for me so I could show in the equitation classes, even though he wasn't an equitation instructor.

We arrived in Kentucky a week before the show and are staying near Tom Moore Stables in Harrodsburg, Kentucky. While at the barn, I saw the most beautiful horses I have ever seen. Mr. Moore has two daughters a few years older than me, and one of them rode a five-gaited pony while we waited. This pony was unreal. Yes, as always, I was dying to ride him but knew I couldn't. I saw several kittens running around too, so while the adults talked, I played with the kittens, walked the halls of the barn, and adventured around outside.

The rolling hills beyond the pastures remind me of large ocean swells. Miles and miles of white-painted wooden fences line each pasture as far as my eyes can see. The pastures divide the horses by age and gender—yearlings with their long, gangly legs that they don't know what to do with yet and two-year-olds, busy figuring out their pecking order within their herds. Elegant broodmares rested underneath the tree branches of huge oak trees with their foals lying flat on the grass, taking their morning naps. There are shades of green and other colors here I have never seen before. The grass has a blue tint, and the tree leaves shimmer and dance in the soft breeze, lit up bright by the blazing sun. The farm is more like a painting than reality! If I wasn't standing, I would have thought I was dreaming, but asleep or awake, I knew I was in some kind of horse heaven. California is so brown in comparison.

When High Hopes was led out of the stall area, I was called into the arena to ride. Mr. Moore reminded us that he wasn't an equitation instructor, but he could help me with the horse. I rode, and Mr. Moore gave me tips and instructions on how to make High Hopes work better.

Pinch me!

After a few days, we left the little town of Harrodsburg and headed to Louisville. Equitation started on the very first day of the show, and the 10 & Under class was first thing in the morning. Nothing seemed familiar—everything was different. Instead of hundreds of horses, there are thousands. The fairgrounds are so large that trainers used golf carts to get from their stalls to the arena. Our California stall drapes and decorations seemed simple compared to what everyone had here. The stall drapes continued down the whole stable's aisle, covering all the stall fronts, and the sitting areas looked like home patios. They had carpet floors or shavings and flowering bushes, and some even had trees lining the sides. Some even had tables with food and bottles of wine or champagne. The only word I can think of is extravagant!

It was hard to sleep the night before my class because of the anticipation and excitement, but it was even harder to wake up. I am not sure if I'm dazed because I'm sleepy or just awestruck by the whole event.

I kept thinking I am a little peanut from California. What am I doing here?

As I trotted into the arena, I could feel the excitement thick in the air, and I heard it in the sound of the bugle calling for our class to enter the arena. The ringmaster played the bugle, a real trumpet, and the sight and sound of this bugle seemed to take hold of my thoughts as it rang around the inside of the huge coliseum. Freedom Hall has over 18,500 seats and bright lights and green shavings. How in the world did they get *green* shavings? The air was cold too—air conditioning! Hundreds of horse people and fair-goers filled the seats starting early in the morning just to see the horse show. It all hit me, my ten-year-old self, like a wave of…fear. I went numb, or maybe it was the freezing cold air conditioning, but silent terror struck me. My mind blanked, and I went into auto-pilot mode. Stage Fright. I don't remember the whole first half of the class. Not at all! After the class, I couldn't have been any prouder of that yellow ribbon—I got third in a huge class. Did I mention there were twenty-four riders from all over the country—all here at Louisville? I must have ridden my pants off the second way because I don't remember any part of the first half of the class. I am so embarrassed, not because of the ribbon, but because I must have looked like a frozen statue. I simply can't remember the first part of the class.

The next morning, I felt more like myself. The new and the scary seemed to fade as I made my way to the warm-up area. Listed in the program were one hundred competitors in this one class, the UPHA challenge cup for riders 17 & Under. The horse show divided this class into four groups to work on the rail, and the top five or six riders from each division would be posted after the classes to see who would qualify for the individual test and perform on the rail as a championship class. After the four classes were over, all the riders walked up to the wall, where the list would be posted outside the show manager's office. I walked through the crowd of riders, the shortest by far, struggling to see among the tall, beautiful girls searching the same paper for their back number. When I found my number, I looked back at Dad and told him I made it, and the tall girl behind me pointed and gasped, saying, "*She* made the cut?"

I scurried away, and Dad and I made our way back to the barn to let Mr. Moore know I would be riding in the next class. Only a few horses were warming up because this was the part of the class where we entered one at a time to execute our pattern work. When my turn came, High Hopes and I entered together showing on the rail, and I rode my tail off. Mom said if I rode like that in my age division class, who knows, maybe I would have won.

Well, that U10 class wasn't my best, but I didn't give up. The organist played High Hopes during the equitation championship class, so I couldn't be happier, and I walked away with two ribbons. I was told I was the youngest juvenile rider from California to place at the World's Championship Horse Show!

*Hallmark Peavine 13396*
*Sketch by Helen K. Crabtree*

## JOURNAL ENTRY: LESSONS FROM A SUPERSTAR

IN THE WINTER MONTHS, SHOW horses take some well-deserved time off. That's Mom's way of saying I will not have lessons on my show horses for a few weeks. However, I do see trainers starting their young horses, and the lesson horses get to teach their old and new riders new tricks. The weather doesn't change too much in California. We know the seasons change when it's time to go back to school. Louisville is now in the past, but I can feel the cold air conditioning hit my face upon entering the arena like it was a moment ago. My teachers are complaining to my mom and dad about the fact that I can only write stories about ponies and horse shows. I don't see the problem. I really don't. Mom surprised me with a trip back to Kentucky to ride and learn from one of the best riding instructors in the world. Plus, I will be getting some last-minute tips before the California Professional Horseman's Association (CPHA) Equitation Finals.

The week at the World's Championship Horse Show in August didn't prepare me for the week at Crabtree

Farm. Mom signed us both up for riding lessons with Mrs. Helen K. Crabtree, and we flew home only to turn around and go back to Louisville a couple weeks later. She is known as the First Lady of Equitation in the American Saddlebred industry and is a world-famous horse trainer. Anne made me promise I would remember everything she taught me and bring it back to California. Probably the only way I could possibly remember everything is to try and write it down though. Mom and I packed our riding pants, boots, gloves, and sweatshirts, and we flew across the country. We were greeted at the baggage claim at the Louisville airport by Mrs. Crabtree herself, who drove us to her farm in her dark green Cadillac. Mrs. Crabtree is a very tall, thin, and elegant woman. She wore jodhpurs, paddock boots, a turtleneck, and a tweed sports jacket; very clean and polished. It didn't look like she came from the barn, working horses.

Crabtree Farm is on Colt Run Road—what a cool name for a road. The farm has black four-board fences lining the pastures along the sides and back of the barn for broodmares and young horses. There is a huge, long red show horse barn with what seemed to be a hundred horse stalls, where a white two-story garage-type building with an upstairs she called "the dormitories" were located. She called it that because her Crabtree girls stay there in the summer months. Next to the dormitories is a pool, but it's closed for the winter months. On the opposite side is a small house she said is the home of the assistant trainer. The main house is a white two-story modest farmhouse where Mr. and Mrs. Crabtree live.

Mom and I stayed in the house, in the rooms where

the Crabtree boy riders live in the summer. When we walked in, we were introduced to Hattie, her cook, who was preparing dinner for all of us. As we walked past the television room, she introduced us to Mr. Charles Crabtree, her husband. She said her son, Redd, is a horse trainer too, but he has a house and barn of his own on the other end of the property. I remembered him because he judged the last horse show of the season in Santa Barbara, California. He is a tall man. As he walked the lineup that day, he was almost face to face with me when I was on Split Second. She led us into a den, which was connected to another room that looked like her office. She sat properly poised in an armchair, looking as if she was about to have her photograph taken. I felt shorter than normal in that moment and sensed I was underdressed. She spoke of horses, world's champions, and people I had never heard of before, but her stories were interesting. The best stories were of her cat, dog, and goat that she had years ago, living at a place called Rock Creek. I liked her. She made me want to sit up tall and listen, but at the same time, she adored all animals, and with that, I knew she was a kind and loving person.

The next morning, we woke up to an empty house, so Mom and I made our way to the barn and walked into the side door, to a lounge or sitting room. We went through it to the other side, to a door that entered into the barn. It was dark and smelled like a strong mix of horses, cedar shavings, and hay. In California, all the barns are open and airy, and we use a white pine wood shaving with less of a scent. This barn has a stronger, mustier smell than I am used to. At the west end of the dark hall, there is a large sliding door. Hiding on the left from view down the aisle, there is another large door that opens to the indoor riding arena. All the doors were closed tight to keep the cold air from freezing water pipes and to help keep the barn warm.

The Crabtree's riding arena is long and narrow, a rectangle shape. It's two-hundred feet long and only fifty feet wide. The walls to the right, or the west side of the arena, have several small windows that only someone sitting on a tall horse could see outside. Needless to say, I couldn't see out the windows. I am not sure even sitting on a horse, my head will reach the window. The east wall shared a wall with the stalls of the back barn. This barn was used for the lesson horses, young horses, and broodmares when they needed to be in a stall. Mrs. Crabtree had an enclosed teaching booth tucked in the northeast corner of the arena, near the large sliding entrance door. There were six small ice cream parlor chairs, her chair, and a microphone propped on a small desk-like area where she sat, and a telephone hung on the wall near her head. She had the perfect view of both sides of the rider, going and coming down the east side rail. This booth is large enough for a few riders to sit with Mrs. Crabtree and watch while the other riders have their lessons. If Anne had a booth like this, she wouldn't be standing all day, nor would she have to yell in order for us to hear her lesson.

In the teaching booth, I sat in silence and watched every move Mom made riding in the arena. I listened intensely, hanging on every word spoken by Mrs. Crabtree. We have two lessons each day, and there is a lot to absorb and remember, but she tape-records each of our lessons for us to be able to study before the next day.

## JOURNAL ENTRY: ADDRESSING REINS

Mrs. Crabtree's riders are expected to "address reins" every time they mount a horse, and she wants me to do the same. The more we do it, the faster it is, and it slowly becomes second nature. In equitation classes, Addressing Reins is test number one in the rule book, and it can be asked of a rider by a judge in the lineup. Anne taught me how to address my reins a couple of years ago, but we didn't practice it until before horse shows. It works like this: the curb bit and snaffle bit each have their own reins, which are buckled together and meeting at the horse whithers. Each rein, each bit, has its own purpose. The trick is in how to control these reins with two hands and make it look easy. Anne taught me what each bit does years ago, so riding with four reins was second nature. My new challenge, though, is addressing my reins without looking down at them or fumbling and doing it swiftly.

## JOURNAL ENTRY: WALKING IN AND OUT OF THE ARENA

I was so embarrassed when Mrs. Crabtree asked me to exit and enter a second time. When I do this wrong, she asks me to do it over until it is done correctly, and today that was me. I had to do it a couple times. I'm supposed to turn to the right using leg aids, walk up and into the corner, and guide my horse to make the turn following the rail, not let my horse simply follow the rail on his own.

Mrs. Crabtree explained why this was important. Every lesson has a purpose, and she talked me through every one of them. "Who is riding whom?" she would ask.

She had a lesson for walking out of the arena as well. If I simply walk straight out the gate at the end of a lesson, this teaches my horse that every time I ride by an open gate, they can exit. And they want to exit! It means they can go back to their stall and be near their friends. It wouldn't be good if I'm riding along and all of a sudden, my horse leaves the arena. Mrs. Crabtree taught me the reason and then the proper way to exit the arena. I'm supposed to walk past the gate using my aids, make a small circle—but not too small—and then exit.

I started thinking about this simple lesson and remembered Coconut and SweetPea trying to leave the arena several times when we were trotting or walking past the gate. Maybe this will stop them from trying to leave the arena at home!

As I sat listening to Mrs. Crabtree, I was starting to feel as if she didn't know I could ride because of the basics she was teaching me. We hadn't even made it around the arena yet, so how could she know. Anne already showed me some of these things, and I have been showing for years. My insides wanted to cry out, but I didn't dare. I sat and listened and learned.

## JOURNAL ENTRY: VOICE COMMANDS

The word "trot," said with meaning in a low but demanding tone, is one of the most important voice commands. Mrs. Crabtree said it is a word a horse can understand,

and they do remember what is being asked of them. It's kind of amazing to think that a horse can understand the English language, but when I squeezed my legs and said, "Trot," this horse trotted off without a cluck or kick. Mrs. Crabtree explained why she doesn't use words for the other gaits, only for the walk, trot, and a "Whoa!" to stop. She also explained why a clucking sound can slowly turn into cricket sounds to a horse. Horses start ignoring that command unless it is used sparingly. She said, "A whip is used to reinforce the authority of your voice command. It acts as an aide to prevent mistakes, not to punish a horse." I like that. It makes me feel more confident in carrying a whip.

## JOURNAL ENTRY: GOOD HANDS

Mrs. Crabtree told me that I have "good hands." She turned to Mom sitting next to her in the teaching booth and told her that the term "good hands" and "light hands" are misused by many people, especially horse trainers. They believe good hands are the ones that have little to no contact with the horse's mouth, but how could a horse possibly know what is expected of them? They must be uncertain until it's too late, and then a jerking or sudden movement happens to their mouth. A somewhat firm, not harsh, and steady pull on the reins builds confidence and makes a horse less likely to sour or get mad. My lesson horse's ears stayed forward, letting Mrs. Crabtree know she was happy. I wasn't pinching her mouth or grabbing the reins harshly, nor was I letting the reins go slack. I heard this on the tape player again in the evening. I guess I didn't realize the importance of good hands before.

The four days were intense. At first, I thought Mrs. Crabtree didn't know I could ride because she was teaching me such basic things, but I started realizing two things. First, she wanted me to understand why I was being asked to do basic things and why she wanted them done a specific way. Secondly, I guess the first time I got on the lesson horse, I was posing instead of riding. I had it wrong about equitation. I thought it was about the rider and how they look. It's actually about the rider's ability to make their horse work to the best of their ability while looking poised and confident. It was important to know that a great rider can take a lesson horse into a show arena and win. I don't want to leave Kentucky. I wanted to learn more from Mrs. Crabtree.

## JOURNAL ENTRY: MAN OVERBOARD WITH EXCITEMENT

SAILING SOUTH FOR CHRISTMAS IS something we have done a few times in the past. We sail down to Baja, California, and sometimes over to Catalina Island for long weekends, when we don't have horse shows or when Dad doesn't have his antique shows to attend. It's sad to leave the animals, but there is something special about sailing on the Pacific Ocean for a few days. Orca whales swim along our hull, but they don't do tricks like you see at Sea World. They normally come up and see what we are, check us out, and then swim off. Once we had dozens circle our boat, and Dad had us get our life vests on and go below deck, into the cabin, where we waited and hoped they didn't want to play with our boat like it was a toy. But they got bored and swam away.

This Christmas, we anchored off the beach in Cabo San Lucas and spent the day snorkeling and surfing behind the dingy. At dinner, DJ and I were surprised by our parents asking, "How would the both of you like to go ride at Crabtree Farms this coming summer?" I about fell out of my seat, but as I looked at DJ, I realized Mom and Dad weren't going to let me go without him. I didn't know how to beg DJ but wished I could.

"When and for how long?" asked DJ.

"We will give the Crabtree's the go-ahead to purchase a new gaited horse for you," Mom said to DJ. Then she turned in my direction and said, "Mrs. Crabtree insists you have a new equitation horse, selected by her."

Horses back east cost the same as a car, so DJ and I both sat stunned at this possibility. After only a few moments, DJ said, "Sure, why not."

My heart skipped a beat, and inside, I screamed and wanted to dance.

# CHAPTER 13



WITH THE WIND IN MY face and Vicky's little legs speeding, galloping just below my feet, we raced along the road. The spring Gladiolus in bloom filled the air with a sweet scent as we made our way closer to the colorful fields. On our latest riding adventure, Vicky and I decided to ride to a new field of flowers growing where the strawberry field was near the bend of the road by Chino's vegetable stand. We seldom planned where to ride. Sometimes, I just let her choose by giving her the reins. The field was filled with Gladiolus flowers almost as tall as I am while sitting on top of Vicky. As we cantered down the rows of various colored flowers, the colors blurred together, almost making a rainbow. It was beautiful! I was lost in the moment, but then soon awakened by the buzzing of bees. We were chased out by angry bees! I don't think I've ever made Vicky gallop so fast.

We made our way home past the dairy farm, where the cows spoke to us, and we crossed the edge of the lima bean field. As we walked, I noticed my feet now dangle near Vicky's knees! I believe she is shrinking. I no longer use a bareback pad or carry a whip, and we no longer canter up the hills or mountains, but we still enjoy a "Hi Ho, Silver" and race along the flat dirt roads. Truly, we are best friends growing up together, exploring the land.

The flowers are proof that spring is here. As soon as school is out for the summer, DJ and I will be getting on a plane and heading to Kentucky. I wish Vicky could be shipped out there with Split Second. It makes me sad to think I will not be riding her the whole summer.

It's just been a few weeks, and it's already time for Split Second to be shipped to Crabtree Farm. DJ and I were told we have two new horses out there too. My new mare's name is Shamrock's Lady Luck, and she's a big bay horse from Atlanta, Georgia. DJ's new five-gaited gelding's name is Bell Hop, and he's a big chestnut, but that's all they could tell us, which just made it more exciting. Mom showed me the plane tickets today. DJ and I will fly to Kentucky the day after school lets out for the summer.

Several of Plaza Del Caballo's Thoroughbred and Saddlebred horses have been sold along with a few others that were in training with Royce. So much is going on, and I am so excited, but I didn't realize how hard it will be to leave. HoneyBear will wonder where I am every night, and Vicky and Coconut might be bored without me. I think Anne is upset, but I reminded myself that as soon as summer and the show season is done, I will be back here to show High Hopes and SweetPea with her.

# CHAPTER 14

## JOURNAL ENTRY: NEW HOUSE RULES

B RIGHT SUNLIGHT BLEEDING THROUGH THE large barn doors helped the florescent lights lighten the dark aisle way. I stood outside Shamrock's Lady Luck's stall after our lesson and watched as Red Tinsley, Shammy's groom and caretaker, reached way over his head to lift my saddle off Shammy's sweaty back.

She is the tallest horse I have ever ridden, and Tinsley isn't that tall of a man, but he seems to like taking care of this big, dark mare. His smile fills his black face, and his whole-body jiggles when he giggles. His laugh and jolly manners remind me of a short African American Santa with black hair. Every morning, he asks how everything is going. No matter how I really feel, I smile back at him and say, "Good." After a while, he reminds me that lunch is waiting for me and tries to scoot me out of the barn. He gives me a second to thank Shammy before he walks her away from me. That has been our typical everyday ritual these past two weeks. I don't want to leave the horses, and he keeps me from getting into trouble.

"Yo' betta get up to the boss's house for lunch," Tinsley warned.

With a pout, I reluctantly turned around and headed toward Mr. and Mrs. Crabtree's house for lunch. Leaving the barn, my eyes burned from the bright light, so I shielded them with my hands and walked across the driveway, through the grassy yard. It was so hot, it looked like the grass was on fire because there was steam rising from the cooler earth as I walked toward the house. In California, I'd spent every hour of sunlight at the barn. I didn't have a set lunchtime like we do at Crabtree Farm.

As I pulled open the house door, a heavenly smell rushed at me. I stepped into the kitchen, and Hattie instantly handed me a plate, smiled, and patted my arm. Hattie is a beautiful black southern lady who is almost as short as I am. She is always cheerful and kind, and she's a great cook. She is the Crabtree Farms chef, and we met her for the first time when Mom and I came for the week-long lesson last November. Silence fell over the kitchen's dining area as if someone turned the radio volume dial down. I could feel the eyes of all the Crabtree riders staring at me as I walked to my seat. Six Crabtree girls and three boy riders, including my older brother DJ, looked up at me and then continued eating their lunches. Late again, but it was hard getting used to handing my reins over to a groom. I don't want to let someone else put my horses away or not be able to watch them. This is close to torture!

Pepper gravy drizzled down both sides of the pile of chicken fried steak and mashed potatoes. I was adding green beans when Mr. Charles Crabtree handed me an envelope. The handwriting was so familiar; one I have known my whole life. I folded the letter and stuffed it in my pocket as Hattie helped me with my plate and sweet tea. My first letter while here at Crabtree Farms this summer, but I wanted to wait to open it so the other girls wouldn't be able to read whatever Mom had written. With my plate in one hand and my sweet tea in the other, I headed for the only open seat that happened to be next to DJ, but he shot me a brotherly look that said to go away. So I plopped my food down at the other end of the table and drug a chair over from the other side.

It's so confusing that in Kentucky, lunch is dinner, and dinner is called supper. No matter what it's called, Hattie's cooking is amazing, and I would eat it any time of day, no matter what they called the meal.

DJ's lesson was with Mr. Crabtree later in the afternoon, so he was able to sleep until noon if he wanted. I always thought he detested riding and practicing. In California, Mom would have to force him to go ride if she could find him. He spent his time riding his motocross bikes, going off to one of his friend's houses, or out to Black Mountain, where there were several dirt bike trails. This is how I end up riding some of his horses, like Dudley Do-Right. My first few lessons on him were due to the fact that DJ couldn't be found, the horse needed to be exercised, and I was still begging for lessons. DJ can get out of almost anything, especially a riding lesson. I wondered why he wanted to come to Kentucky with me, so I asked him. He told me he likes showing horses—the showing off part at the horse shows, anyway—and hanging out with all the other riders at the horse shows. Plus, he really likes Bell Hop. He hasn't complained at all about lessons here, and I think he really likes Mr. Crabtree.

Mr. Crabtree is Bell Hop's trainer, and I don't think DJ's disappearing act will be easy here. Plus, DJ wants to show Bell Hop. He is a really cool horse. It doesn't matter how many horses I am showing, I can't help it, I always want to ride his horse. It's not only DJ's horses, though. It's all horses. I watch them move, their power, and wonder how they feel. I've always been curious about other horses, all horses, but especially my brother's horses. It's a strange feeling, and I can't help it.

Not opening my letter at lunch ended up being a good decision because I wasn't ready for the other girls to see the magazines with me in it. A copy of the "Saddle Horse Report," a horse show magazine page, was neatly folded inside the envelope. There was a huge picture of me mounted on my equitation horse, High Hopes, taken at the Carousel Horse Show only weeks ago. The article read: "Starting the 1979 season in the winner's circle. Eight Shows – Eight blues at the Carousel Horse Show." The article listed my horse show wins, along with the names of my horses and ponies, plus my family and trainers. I realized, for probably the first time, that I rode and showed a lot in California! As far as I know, the other girls here don't know how much I showed, nor did they know what classes I showed in. It is probably best to keep that to myself.

The other Crabtree girls walked out and headed toward the dorm, probably on their way to the pool by now. It's steamy outside, and they didn't have another lesson today, so they could go relax in the pool for the afternoon.

I unfolded the letter to read the second page in the envelope. It's from a different horse magazine, and the headline read, "RuthAnne, the youngest rider to win almost everything in the juvenile division on the west coast!" Those words make me proud, but at the same time, a little intimidated here in Simpsonville, Kentucky, the heart of the Saddlebred industry. Riding with the top Saddlebred trainers in the world and against the top riders in the world, I'd better buckle up, Buttercup. I might have been well known in California, but here, I feel like a little fish in the big deep ocean, and I just went big time. I folded the magazine page and letter up, stuffed it back into the envelope, and pushed it deep into my jodhpur pocket as I headed toward the barn, following on the heels of Mr. Crabtree.

We have been here for over two weeks, and this is my first day to get a lesson from Mr. Charles Crabtree on Split Second. Split Second arrived last week from Royce's barn. That must have been a long drive while standing up. I can't imagine how tired Split Second must have been. Mr. Crabtree wants to see how we work together before he puts a lot of training into him. My heart fluttered in my chest, or was that my gut? I couldn't help the feeling of pure excitement. A lesson with Mr. Charles Crabtree, another trainer who has won so many world's championship titles, I bet he can't count them all.

As I waited, I thought about how I had never ridden Split Second for anyone besides Royce Cates, so I guess I was a bit anxious. Tinsley led Split Second out of his stall for me, stopped him, and pulled down the stirrups, and we exchanged our usual small talk. Tinsley always asks,

"You ready?" As for Split Second, I think he was happy to see me. He turned his head to look at me when I spoke. That little look made me happy, but Tinsley made him look forward again before he walked back to his side to give me a leg up. I was full of nerves, mainly excited and very curious about how Mr. Crabtree teaches. After the lesson, it was shocking how different his lessons seemed to be from Mrs. Crabtree's lessons, but they both teach so much, it's hard to take it all in. Though I do see why DJ likes to ride with Mr. Crabtree so much. Mr. Crabtree is fun. He makes you think and challenges your knowledge, but at the same time, he makes it exciting to get the most from your horse. When we were done, Tinsley walked us back to the stall. Even though my lesson was over, Tinsley's work had just begun. Split Second was a sweaty mess, and I felt bad that I couldn't stay at the barn to help him wash Split Second off or walk him to cool him out.

## JOURNAL ENTRY: DOGS, CATS, AND PONIES

Most people think horse farms have dogs and cats to keep rodents away, but I think they are here to love—un-conditionally—the trainers, riders, caretakers, and even the horses. Several nights in the dormitories, when I get ready for bed, I get a little sad. I wish I had HoneyBear to sleep with me. Not all riders are lucky to have a horse like Shammy that will actually hug back. When I wrap my arms around her chest, Shammy curls her long neck around my shoulder and rests her jaw on my other shoulder, giving me a squeeze. But at night, I can't go in the stall for a Shammy hug. It's the most calming feeling to feel love from an animal.

It's hard to even write HoneyBear's name without feeling sad—not grief, but very lonely because she is still at home in California. This summer in Kentucky has been awesome so far, but I miss her snuggles at night. Her favorite spot to sleep is on the top of my head! I pleaded with Mom to let me bring her with me, but I didn't win. The dorm room is lonely, especially when I start thinking of her. I guess that's part of the reason why I write notes and journal. It helps me remember my riding lessons and takes some of the lonely feelings away.

The Crabtrees' dogs follow their every move like little shadows. It's funny to watch their dogs' eyes, especially when either Mr. or Mrs. Crabtree mount a horse. Ben, their Bull Dog, is the funniest. He will follow Mr. Crabtree down the hall, into the arena, watch him start to ride, pout a little, and then leave in search of Mrs. Crabtree. If they both are riding or in the arena at the same time, Ben pouts. Seriously, he drops his head almost to the ground and practically drags his bottom lip on the dirt, then he flops down outside the arena, usually along the side of a stall door, and he waits and sleeps. Somehow, he hears them dismount and then bounces to full attention, from a snore to all fours. Ben resumes following either of them from the house to the barn, to the car for a ride to the post office, and everywhere in between. If he could follow them both at the same time, he would be the happiest dog alive. That's true love.

I don't have a dog, but Vicky follows me everywhere. It's sometimes better when I am holding the lead rope though. My four-legged shadow has hooves. Her favorite food is Jujubes candies, and if I have a box of those, she will follow me anywhere, even without a lead rope. When I was about five, Mom and Dad were not at home, and I decided it was time for my best outside friend to meet my best inside friend. This meeting would take place inside the house, and the bonus was that Vicky would get to see my stall, or as we call it, my room. Up the stairs and down the hall we went, and as Vicky and I entered my room, HoneyBear took one look at Vicky, jumped straight up into the air, and ran for the nearest hiding place she could find—under the bed. This spooked Vicky, so she tried to turn around in my entrance, which is a hall with a closet only a couple feet wide. She hit the closet doors, which caused a banging sound and scared her even more. I pulled on her halter, begging her to go farther into my room, and finally got her turned around. She led me back down the hall to the stairs and then refused to go any farther. Even though she was scared of the whole "meet HoneyBear" thing, she didn't want to go down the steps. I had to leave her in the house, all by herself.

No matter how much trouble I was going to be in, I needed help. My grandmother always said, "The bravest thing you can ever do is ask for help." But at that moment, I was the biggest chicken of all time. Vicky being stuck inside the house was more than I could handle. I didn't want to give up, but asking for help isn't giving up. We're supposed to ask for help when we need it. Right? I had to run all the way down to the barn, talk someone into coming up to help me, and then when they realized how stuck Vicky was, they went back to the barn for more help. Soon, everyone at the barn was in the house trying to figure out how to get Vicky down the stairs. It was not my brightest hour. Mom arrived back from running her errands, a bit surprised to see all the horse trainers and grooms from the barn in the house, trying to get Vicky down the stairs. By this time, I knew how much trouble I was going to be in, but after Vicky was safely back in her corral, I was the one who was panicked and worried. I didn't get in huge trouble, but I sure learned a lesson or two.

After my lesson tomorrow, I think I will go search for the Crabtree kittens in the back barn. Maybe they will come out and play with me.

## JOURNAL ENTRY: IS SOUTHERN ANOTHER LANGUAGE?

There are times when it sounds as if I am in a foreign country instead of Kentucky. Sometimes, the grooms tease me for saying things like a Californian, but there are many times I can't understand them. When Red Tinsley introduced himself to me, I had to ask a couple times what his name is until he finally said, "This color." He pointed to his red-colored Crabtree Farm shirt. It sounded like "ray-ed" or "raid." From one embarrassing moment to the next, I've been asking DJ to translate if I'm not sure. Needless to say, I call him Tinsley.

Tinsley: Zat yo horse?

Me: Her name is Shammy, not Zat.

Tinsley: Ah'm too tarred to wuk.

Me: (no comment)

Tinsley: Yo momma gonna wear you out if you do dat to yo breeches.

Me: (clueless)

Tinsley: Is DJ ugly to you?

Me: He's my brother, so yes, he's ugly and yucky.


The grooms would say, "Just pickin'," and I would say, "Picking what?" Again, they were only teasing me, this time with a phrase that also means teasing me. It was infuriating, but also very funny.

Apparently, the word "awraht" can be either a question or a statement, but first, what is "awraht?" Translating southern for me has been done on the down-low by DJ, and he explained it meant "all right." These jumbled words are getting the best of me, and I have only been here a couple of weeks. I'm not sure why understanding this southern language comes so easy for DJ and not me.

The more I hang out around the barn, the more I pick up and really enjoy spending time with the grooms. They all think how I talk is funny, to my surprise. I didn't think Californians had an accent.

Paula, another Crabtree rider my age, has a southern accent! I can understand what she is saying, so maybe the problem is just hearing in the barn. When Dad comes to watch a horse show, he says, "Paula is not only the sweetest girl, but she has a great sense of humor." He's convinced Paula to teach him Southern whenever he's in town. She sits down with him outside the tack room at the barn and slowly explains to my "dense" father how to speak and understand southern. The funny thing is that the more she teaches him, the more I am learning. One day, Paula gave Dad a book called *How to Speak Southern, Book One* by Steve Mitchel. When she handed it to him, she told him to study it and then she would explain anything he still didn't understand. At the next horse show, he asked Paula something, and when she spoke, he said, "Wait a minute. Let me get out this book and see if I can translate what you just said to me." I wasn't sure whether to hide from embarrassment or cry with laughter, but they laughed so hard together, causing my dad to laugh so hard that he had tears in his eyes.

They went on like this every horse show, and I am sure it will never get old to my dad. He will never stop. I'm not sure if this is funny or insulting. If insulting, I don't know who it's insulting, but it should be my dad. Dad and Paula have fun with this game. I am starting to understand southern more. I overhear the grooms and can understand more, even when they place bets with one another while they don't think anyone can hear them, or in my case, they don't think I can understand them.

I hope ya'll know I'm becoming more fluent in Southern. I am also finding that southern girls are sweet as pie and southern boys are super polite. The boys always say things like "Yes, ma'am" or "No, Sir" while looking straight into people's eyes, especially while speaking with an adult. Looking into people's eyes is not a strong suit of my own. My whole body becomes weak, my face flushes, and the need to take flight overwhelms me.

## JOURNAL ENTRY: GROOMS & CARETAKERS

In California, because of my petite size and being between

the ages of five and ten, I didn't do near the things other older riders at Rancho Del Mar did for themselves. They groomed their horses and saddled them before every lesson and before classes at a horse show. However, if I was heading off on a trail ride on one of my ponies, I was expected to do everything. I spent countless hours rubbing them down, grooming Vicky and Coconut. I would take them into the arena for countless hours for pretend shows. I followed my mom and anyone else who had a lesson and would play "horse show." When I started showing, Anne and her grooms would take care of the horses. In Kentucky, it's not much different, but there are unspoken rules that I have had to learn by watching other riders, and Tinsley helps me with the rules around the stalls. It's the "Crabtree ways," as Tinsley says. He made everything easy for me by making me and my horses look perfect, and for that, I am so thankful. I'm not to "spoil" my horses, but he lets me sneak in to hug Shammy when he goes to get something from the tack room and takes a second longer than he probably needed to. There is a checklist, longer than my arm, of things he has to do to prepare our horses and make sure we are ready as well. I wasn't aware of half of these things until he showed me. The better your horse's groom, the better they make you look as a team. Since I was little, I think I have taken the work grooms and caretakers do for granted. I hope I didn't take them for granted, but I should try and think of a way to thank them.

I don't think it would be possible without our horses' caretakers. Maybe it would be, but our trainers would be beyond exhausted. No, it's not possible, unless a trainer had only a few horses, and the owners would have to help a lot. I need to thank all the grooms. If it wasn't for them, I wouldn't be at Crabtree's, nor would we look as polished. I know Tinsley is always there for me, and if he isn't, Mike, Raymond, or any of the other grooms are there when we need them. Which is always.

## JOURNAL ENTRY: LESSON SCHEDULES

Mrs. Crabtree gives all of her riders a specific time to be at the barn and ready for lessons. I've had early lessons since I've arrived, I guess so I can have extra time teaching Shammy patterns and getting used to all the Crabtree ways. It is our responsibility to be at the barn on time, which means to be early, dressed, and ready to ride. Every morning, I wake up early to the crazy sound of a buzzing alarm clock. I tip-toe down the dorm hallway to the bathroom, located next to the older riders' dorm rooms, knowing I have to be quiet because I don't want to wake the others who have a good hour more of sleep before they have to be at the barn. I brush my teeth, braid my long, curly hair, change into a T-shirt, my jodhs, and my paddock boots, then head down to the barn. The sun isn't even awake! I hear the horses munching on their breakfast, the barn smell hits me, and then I feel at home. Kentucky barns smell stronger than in California because of the cedar shavings, but it's becoming normal and very comforting.

This morning, a few "good mornings" were heard as I scurried my way to Shammy's stall. Shammy is the perfect nickname for Shamrock's Lady Luck because her coat feels as soft as a shammy, or softer, like the fur on a mink. Yes, her coat is amazingly silky. I gave her a morning hug and rubbed her shoulder. Then Tinsley arrived with her bridle in his hand and shooed me out of the stall. I watched in amazement how this short man could slip the bridle on her with such ease. As I thought this, Shammy's head drifted higher, as if she were aiming toward the barn rafters. Tinsley moved slow and gentle, spoke softly to her, and rubbed her forehead, which she seemed to love, and then she allowed him to slip the curb and snaffle bits into her mouth. He secured the bridle over her ears and moved his hands swiftly but gently, making his way around the bridle, fastening straps and the curb chain under her chin, making sure nothing was pinching her skin, and tucking all the leather strap ends securely into their holders.

We both gave her a pat on her neck, then Tinsley moved me out of the stall again. He led her into the dimly lit barn aisle, preparing her for my ride. After a couple last adjustments on Shammy's tack, Tinsley grinned at me. I turned toward Shammy and reached up with my arms, holding the reins in my left hand and the back flap of my saddle with my right. I can't hold the back of the saddle because Shammy is so tall. Matter of fact, I can hardly reach the stirrups from the ground! At least, I would have a hard time adjusting my stirrups if I needed to change their length. Tinsley reached down for my left leg, hold-ing onto my left shin to lift me onto her back. One, two, three! I bounced up with my right leg landing softly on her back. Automatically, my feet found my stirrups, but Tinsley removed them and wiped off my dusty boots, pulled my cuffs down, and wiped my pant legs off as I addressed my reins. Then Tinsley held the stirrup, allowing my foot to slide right in. He proceeded to our right side to repeat the same task of cleaning my boot and pant leg. Ever since my week with Mom visiting Crabtree's, I have practiced every day when riding with a double bridle and addressing my reins. It's becoming much easier, and I am getting fast.

I know I've only been a Crabtree girl for a couple weeks, but I am learning so much from Mrs. Crabtree and have to admit, I am learning a lot from Tinsley and the other riders too. Mrs. Crabtree teaches me that every move has a meaning and every lesson has a purpose, and she explains the 'why' in such detail that it sinks in while practicing. I ride, then I write, and then… Yes, I ride in my sleep. I dream about the good and the bad, and sometimes I have some crazy weird rides in my sleep. I even dreamt that Shammy and I trotted into a class, and as I went around the arena, I started noticing I'd forgotten things. First, I noticed we forgot the saddle. Then a few moments later, I noticed I wasn't wearing my riding habit, then I was holding a lead rope because we forgot her bridle, and that's when I finally woke up. Maybe these dreams are happening because we are about to head to our first horse show together soon. I can't wait, but at the same time, I am a bit nervous. Okay, terrified!

The sound system popped on inside the arena, startling Tinsley and I both. Even Shammy had her ears forward, looking to see what was scary at the end of the hall. Tinsley made sure my tie-downs were in place. The elastic and leather straps sometimes come off, but they are supposed to be attached to the inside of each pant leg. He stretched the band underneath—in front of my boot's heel—from one side to the other and buttoned the side that came undone. Then he pulled a whip from his back pocket and handed it to me. It was very important to be on time, looking like a tailored Crabtree rider even behind closed doors, and always ride like you are in the show arena. I am beginning to see the importance of these tiny details, inside and outside of the arena, but trying to apply them at the crack of dawn, before I am fully awake, is still a challenge.

## JOURNAL ENTRY: SHOPPING WITH MRS. CRABTREE

Showing in California, I had one riding suit, and Mom only purchased a new one if I outgrew it. I didn't need a spare. The one suit worked for all of my classes, and I showed a lot! From riding and driving SweetPea in the combination classes to an equitation class—or a three-gaited class, a five-gaited class, and even evening classes or morning classes—one suit. That was it. I never thought about what would happen if it got torn. I guess we would sew it. Now thinking about it, it's almost as if they appeared from the riding attire gods because I don't remember going anywhere to try suits on or get them fitted. It didn't matter where they came from as long as I could show my horses and ponies.

When I arrived here in Kentucky, Mrs. Crabtree wanted to see my horse show riding attire. She needed to know what I needed before we headed off to our first horse show together. Mom flew in to see us for a couple days and brought my riding clothes. She handed me my suit bag, boots and hatbox, and I went into the bathroom to change. When I came out, and Mrs. Crabtree saw me… Let's put it this way, I have never seen a woman or trainer so upset over horse riding clothes. Mom and I watched Mrs. Crabtree inspect my suit, repeatedly gasping and saying, "This will not do. It will not work." Then Mom and Mrs. Crabtree talked while I went to change. I hung up the suit and walked into Mrs. Crabtree's office, where she was talking on the phone. Apparently, we were going shopping!

We drove about an hour and a half to Lexington to see a professional tailor named Nicholas. He makes custom horse show riding habits for Mrs. Crabtree's customers. There is a suit for equitation, a suit for five-gaited, and a tuxedo for the evening three-gaited and for equitation evening classes. Mom questioned Mrs. Crabtree about why all these suits were necessary for one rider while the tailor measured every inch of my legs, arms, neck, back, waist, and even my feet. We looked at rolls and swatches of beautiful fabric that would soon be my riding habits while Mrs. Crabtree explained the importance. She said I not only need to ride like a world-class athlete, but I need to look like a world's champion. As I felt the soft wool fabric, I could tell these were going to be high-quality suits, but I had no idea how much they would cost— maybe several hundreds of dollars each. Mrs. Crabtree even chose the liner and vest color. The vest, she said, would "pop" and bring another reason for people to take notice. My new equitation suit was to be kept a secret and unveiled at a horse show. She said that the color of my equitation riding habit will be the lightest color worn by any equitation rider. She added that a light color will show all the movement in a leg and all the flaws of a rider, but she knew my legs were set in place and strong, and she wanted to show them off to everyone. Mrs. Crabtree picked a beautiful light gray-colored material to be lined with a rich chocolate-colored lining, with a dark brown vest. My accessories—the hat, boots, whip, and gloves— were going to be dark brown, and I would wear a crisp white shirt. I felt the excitement with all of these changes and expectations, but I was also beginning to feel nervous! She chose navy blue for my tuxedo and a light brown/tan for my five-gaited habit. Mom took out her checkbook and handed the tailor the deposit.

While in Lexington, we drove to a store called Carl Meyers. This place had everything a horse rider would ever need and more. The walls were lined with derby hats, top hats, and homburg hats the men show in, which are like the bowler or derby hats but have a gutter crown that looks like a dent. They remind me of the dents in a cow-boy hat. DJ wears one to show in, and so do all the men trainers. This place has drawers filled with leather riding gloves for men, women and children, and paddock boots of all sizes and colors. They even have shiny boots that are called patent leather, and they are used with the tuxedo riding suits and the three-gaited and equitation evening or night classes. Every time I turned around, I saw a new section of accessories in different sizes and colors, plus several suit colors I've never seen used in the show ring before.

We were there to buy boots—brown and black boots for day, and black patent leather boots for the tuxedo—

black, white, and brown gloves, tie-downs to hold pant legs down—two pairs in black, brown, and an extra pair for my practice jodhs. In the hat section, we chose a brown derby and a dark blue top hat for the navy-colored tuxedo. Both felt too tight, but she assured me this was to keep the hat on top of my head while riding. We moved to the shirt section, and she chose two wing tip shirts for the tuxedo, black buttons for the tuxedo shirts, a chocolate-colored shirt for the gaited suit, and a white shirt for the equitation suit. Everything was measured, fitted, tried on, snug, and proper. Snug was an understatement, and I was so worried about how tight Mrs. Crabtree wanted my shirt collar to be. She said a finger, only a finger, should slide between your neck and the collar. I didn't have a finger that skinny and thought maybe I would pass out right then and there, and my head still hurts from the squeeze of my hats. I had no idea what a proper fit is until today!

Mrs. Crabtree chose two bow ties, one white and one navy, and a couple suit ties—one gray for the equitation suit, and a deep red tie and matching red boutonnière for my five-gaited suit. We even purchased two really nice whips—one black and one brown—and until riding at Crabtree's, I didn't use a whip. I could only imagine the speed I would get if I used a whip with Split Second. He would get going and never stop. Mrs. Crabtree says that the use of a whip is an aid to prevent mistakes rather than a punishment and should always be carried. This reminded me, I always carried a whip when I started riding Vicky. If I had it in my hand, she never acted up. If I forgot it, Vicky knew, and our ride ended up in a fight over who's the boss. Today's shopping bonus: I have new practice jodhpur's and gloves. Maybe Tinsley won't have to fix my tie-downs every time I get on.

Mrs. Crabtree's Cadillac was loaded with hatboxes, boot boxes, and bags of accessories, and this didn't include the suits the tailor would make and send later. I listened to Mrs. Crabtree as she spoke about me on the ride home. She said some of the nicest things I have ever heard, and to come from Mrs. Crabtree! I was overwhelmed with honor. I also heard all of the things I need to work on and improve. I have to prove to her that I can rise to this challenge; work my tail off to be as good of a rider as she said I can be.

Everything is so different here, but so very exciting. I learned today that a neatly-fitted suit, all the accessories, the right colors—the "small stuff"—can make a huge difference. The riding habit will not make me a better rider. It will only give me the appearance of being a swan—beautiful on the outside and working like crazy to make the whole picture look good underneath it all. Mom learned how much riding habits and accessories cost. She made a comment about needing to go sell something before she could pay the rest of the bill, and I felt overwhelmed with appreciation, but I also hoped she wasn't going home to sell Vicky.



Today, I walked into the riding arena with a purpose. Show ready! However, I wasn't sure why I was having another lesson behind closed doors, early in the morning before the other equitation riders got out of bed. I hadn't had a group lesson since I arrived and wondered why, but I never, ever questioned Mrs. Crabtree's decisions. The barn door was slid shut behind me, which I heard and felt without looking back, and it made me nervous because I wasn't sure what the purpose of shutting the door was exactly. Mrs. Crabtree checked her microphone, and the speakers blared over my head at different spots in the arena, then she turned her volume down and began teaching. From the gait of a walk, to the transitions into the trot, back to the walk, and into a canter, everything was a lesson. And with every lesson, she explained what she was seeing, what she wanted to see, and why. Mrs. Crabtree explained everything, sometimes multiple times but in different ways. I started realizing this is how she teaches everyone from the past couple of weeks while sitting in the booth with her, listening to the others' lessons. Why it is important to walk sitting tall, heels down, hands up, elbows in, looking straight between your horse's ears. Why we need to shorten our reins in every corner and always pay attention to what is happening underneath us.

I can now see out the windows in the arena while sitting on Shammy because she is so tall, but I only look with my eyes. I never turn my head to look out the window. As I was preparing for the trot, it was a full-fledged mind assault, from my mind to every part of my body it was working. Feeling Shammy's stride, the right shoulder moving forward, and then the left. Mindful of her hind end, is it following straight or did I need to square her body? Is her head high enough? Are my reins short enough, or do I need to wiggle and slide my reins through my fingers quickly to get a little more hold of her head?

Shortening the reins, pushing down in my heels, saying "Trot," pressing my thighs tight into my saddle while never forgetting what shoulder and what leg is moving forward so I can come up trotting on the correct diagonal. The fence was on my right side, so this meant my body should go up when her right leg moves forward. Following her walk shoulder pattern made it easy for me to rise out of my saddle when I needed. I never stop thinking, and if I did, Mrs. Crabtree would somehow know even on the other side of the long arena. She can read a horse's body language like a book—the twitch of an ear, how they respond to a rider, or even how they are reacting to a bit in their mouth. I figure if I can keep in tune with my horse's mind and body, Mrs. Crabtree would be able to know, and it makes it feel as if Shammy and I have become synced into one.

No one was in the arena except me. No one to judge me. No one to see how hard I was working. No one to see how many times we had to repeat figure eights, straight lines, and serpentines. Except for Mrs. Crabtree. She was the only one I had to impress. But there was no one else to see how many times I simply needed to start and stop again—at the trot, canter, and even the walk—to keep Shammy's body straight on the imaginary line drawn somewhere in the arena or on the rail. We had quiet time to let Shammy stop so we could praise her for her hard work and let her take a breath. She lowered her head, and I felt her body relax underneath me. Even that time was a time to learn; to see how Shammy was taking all the work in. I was teaching her! But was I teaching her bad habits?

Her body language at a relaxed halt told so much. I

could only slightly see Mrs. Crabtree in her booth because of the glass window she sat behind, but I knew she was staring at us and thinking. The silence was deafening, but also sweet. She was teaching me how to train a horse, or at least how to do patterns properly. It is surreal being here in Kentucky and doing what I love most. I hope I never wake up from this dream.

Mrs. Crabtree told me I would start riding with the others after our first horse show. For now, I need all her attention to get caught up with everyone else.

# CHAPTER 15

JOURNAL ENTRY: A MISFIT GIRL

A FTER ONLY A COUPLE WEEKS of training and getting to know Shamrock's Lady Luck, we are already
heading to a horse show. Even though Indio and The
Carousel Horse Shows were only a few weeks ago, they
are slipping away like a distant California memory. I've
been on a crash learning course with Mrs. Crabtree, and it
feels like months have passed. DJ and I are riding to Ohio
with Mrs. Crabtree in her Cadillac. DJ fell asleep while
Mrs. Crabtree was telling me stories. She warned me that
I should consider this a practice show, but said she expects
me to ride like I do at Crabtree Farms. Her firm warnings
were:

- If the mare does anything wrong, slowly correct
  her.

- The most important thing is to not let anything
  frighten her.

- We need to make sure Shammy has a good first
  experience in the show ring with me.

I hadn't seen Shammy prior to owning her, but I know she was shown. Mrs. Crabtree said that she wished my riding suit was ready but reassured me that everything would be fine. I think she was trying to convince herself more than me because I have been wearing this suit all spring, and it seemed fine to me.

Bell Hop is a super cute horse, but I don't dare call him cute in front of DJ or he'll punch me in the arm. Bell Hop looks big, powerful, and fun. Those simple descriptive words drive my curiosity of wanting to know how he feels to ride even more! Where Split Second, my gaited horse, is built like a mare, slender and fine, he has the speed of a bullet. I know I've said this before, but boy does he like to go fast! DJ and I are in different age divisions for the qualifying classes, then we have to show against each other in the championship. In the championship classes, we would typically be tied first and second in the championships when he was showing Secret Call. It just depended on who had the better ride. I am sure he will beat me with Bell Hop, but I will always give him a run for his money. I am just thrilled Split Second was good enough to come with me so we can show in five-gaited classes. I wouldn't know what to do with myself if I only had one horse to show. I can't wait to get to Cincinnati.

It's surreal being at the Crabtree Farms showing in Cincinnati, Ohio for a horse show. When we pulled up, the security guard already knew Mrs. Crabtree and waved us in the gate. She was allowed to park near the stable area. The arena is on a horse racetrack. The horses being led out of their stalls are beautiful, and all of the barns have fancy stable fronts with sitting areas and plants set up like a flower garden. It makes the drab old Cincinnati race track barns look colorful, fancy, and, I guess, professional. It's not as fancy as Louisville though. They must have left all that fancy stuff at home to save it for the World's Championship Horse Show. Golf carts and other electric buggies are used by the horse trainers to get back and forth from the stable areas to the show arena, and most of them are painted in stable colors or have the stable logo painted on the sides. It makes me think of all the walking Anne did in California at the shows, back and forth from the stable area to the show ring, before she purchased a golf cart.

Mrs. Crabtree walked me up the show ring, and as we stood watching, the tractor drove around dragging the surface, flattening the dirt and making it safer for the horses to show. She looked at me and asked me several different questions like if I had my marks yet, if I saw the spots where my horse might have issues, did I see anything that might scare her, and she asked me how I planned on riding in the ends of the arena because they were narrow. Frankly, no! I was watching the tractor. I think by the blank look on my face, she knew that I hadn't, so she helped me by talking me through it all, then she left me there for a few minutes to find my marks and figure it out. When she came back from the horse show office, I pointed my marks out to her, and she adjusted them for me and explained how to spot them while in the arena. She helped me with estimating the steps and strides it would take to get from one mark to the next. She explained to me that even though my first class was performed on the rail, this is always the first thing you do when you come to a horse show, even if you've showed there before. Have a plan, be organized, and practice even if the practice is in your head, and then practice more. She also said, "Watch the other classes. See if you can spot any issues in the show ring where horses are breaking out of their gaits or avoiding. Maybe something is scaring them like someone's hat or a flag waving. Be aware of it all, and be prepared for anything." I really wish someone had done this with me before my class at Louisville for the World's Championship Horse Show. Maybe I wouldn't have frozen the first half of my equitation age division class on High Hopes.

Back at the stables, Mrs. Crabtree kept sending me back to the sitting area, away from my horse's stalls, but being near the horses is where I feel most comfortable and relaxed. As much as Mrs. Crabtree didn't want me to see Shammy back in the stalls, it was important to me to connect with her, I guess to let her know I am here with her. All the girls were getting ready for our equitation age group classes, hustling in and out of the dressing room with their moms. Mrs. Crabtree noticed me standing around, half ready. She didn't say a word. She simply started going to work on me, getting me ready to show. She took my braid down and was trying to put my hair in a bun, borrowing a hairnet from one of the other riders to help keep my curly hair from flying away, all the while teaching me how and why we need black electrical tape around the tops of our boots and gloves. She pinned my number on my show jacket and told me the reason why we did this, then she borrowed someone's makeup and proceeded to show me how to apply it for the arena.

This is not what we did in California! Pins in my hair were stabbing my scalp, causing a serious headache. Okay, Mom did do the same thing, but she didn't put this nasty hair spray on to keep every hair in place. Maybe it was my really tight-fitted derby, my shirt collar, or tie, but something was making me feel nauseous. I was afraid I was going to puke and needed to sit. Today, Mrs. Crabtree was teacher, trainer, and Mom all rolled into one for me, and I'm not complaining! But it was hard to hide my face turning green when it felt like I was riding a really fast spinning ride at a fair. Boy, I'm glad I sat down quickly.

All the Crabtree riders looked glamorous, so very pristine and simply perfect. I, on the other hand, noticed that I looked out of place and started feeling very self-conscious. I had never been this nervous before a class—ever! As Mrs. Crabtree made sure everyone was ready for all the different age groups, I felt better and snuck off to stay close to Shammy. Tinsley listened to the paddock announcer and prepared to lead Shammy out of her stall. He asked me for my whip, tucked it in his back pocket, grabbed a clean rag, then he led Shammy out of her stall. I couldn't believe how beautiful she looked. Her coat was almost black, her tack was sparkling clean, her hooves polished, her tail glistened—every part of her was so clean and shiny. She was a stunning sight as she walked onto the dirt road where I was to get on her. She held her head high and her ears forward as if to say, "I'm ready." I wished I felt the same.

Mrs. Crabtree had already headed to the ring with the 10 & Under riders about thirty minutes prior, so Mr. Crabtree gave me a leg up onto Shammy's back while

Tinsley held her. I addressed my reins as Tinsley walked around us like he did every day at the barn, shining us both up. Then he handed me my whip, and we were ready to head to the warm-up arena for our class. I followed Mr. Crabtree to the warm-up arena as Tinsley walked beside me with his grooming kit. I felt like a million dollars on this horse, but knew I looked like someone they found on the side of the road, a misfit. Tinsley smiled at me and told me the big boss, Mr. Crabtree, was leading the way and would warm us up. "This must be a special day for you and Shammy." I might have dismissed his remarks because I felt out of sorts, knowing my riding suit didn't look as new as everyone else's. They didn't have pinstripes and a matching vest, and it looked worn. I felt so out of place. I sat comparing myself to others, and it was stripping all of my confidence away.

We entered the crowded warm-up area on my sixteen-two-hand mare. I felt small, not only in size on top of Shammy, but how I felt in this grand company of these top riders. As we continued to walk into the arena, I noticed people had stopped what they were doing, and dozens of eyes were on me and this beautiful mare. I heard whispers but didn't process one word. I hoped they were wondering why Mr. Crabtree was bringing a rider to an equitation class, but I knew better.

Mrs. Crabtree arrived after the 10 & Under class ribbons were being announced and shortly before calling our class of seventeen horses into the arena. Mr. Crabtree told her that I had cantered up and back on the rail but hadn't trotted a step.

Mrs. Crabtree said, "Perfect." She came over to us,

adjusted Shammy's curb chain and ran her hand over her bridle. She looked at me and whispered, "Don't listen to anyone, do you hear me?"

I nodded and held back a swell of nervous emotions, hoping not to cry, while she continued.

"Ride exactly how you did at our farm and you will be perfect, or I would not have brought you here. You will trot up toward the show ring. They will open the gate for you as you approach it, so just continue at the trot and trot right in. Go straight! Then make your way to the rail. Be the first horse in the arena and make that judge see you!" She patted my leg and said, "Now, go have fun! Go, now, trot!"

As the 10 & Under winner made her way out of the arena on her victory pass, I started at the trot toward the closed entrance gate. As I approached, the gatekeeper quickly swung the gate open so I didn't need to slow. I heard DJ's voice as I was entering into the ring, "Kick butt, Annie." For some reason, this made my nerves disappear and I started to ride!

As the announcer called rider's ages eleven through fourteen into the ring, my new dark bay mare and I had already stepped into the arena, now for the first time, with her high stepping elegant trot. I could feel her lift her head and tense a little not because of nerves, but with excitement. With a low tone of voice, and between the smile I always wear while riding, I firmly said, "Trot." From the moment I entered the ring, I believed *everyone*—hundreds of spectators and dozens of horse trainers—were watching us. Even though I was looking straight forward between my mare's ears, I could feel hundreds of sets of eyes on the new "Crabtree girl." Everything felt perfect, except I knew I wasn't looking…well, very Crabtree-stylish.

Each stride Shammy took, the bond between us seemed to grow. She was counting on me, and I was guiding her every step. Everything disappeared in the ring. I could only hear Mr. and Mrs. Crabtree's voices and Shammy's hooves hitting the ground, Shammy's breathing, and the announcer's request for our next gait. Mrs. Crabtree's voice came like a whisper in my ear. "That a girl!" The other horses in the class had followed me into the arena, and I was aware of each horse's location in the ring. It was up to me not to allow them to cover me up from the judge's sight, cut me off, or get too close to upset my horse. I needed to keep them looking as if they were following me. I knew how to space myself in the arena, to be seen, but today, the blue—the win—wasn't the purpose. Today, Shammy and I were going to be put through several tests. Not the figure eight kind, but seeing if we trusted each other, what needed to be improved upon, what training worked, and what needed improving besides our pattern work that we already know needs work. The class was called to the lineup, and I was instructed to find Mrs. Crabtree on the rail and face her. When our eyes met, she looked so serious. Shammy felt great and didn't seem to mind all the horses in the arena. After the judge walked the lineup and judging was complete, I reached down and gave Shammy a pat on her shoulder. I felt her take a deep breath and relax.

My number being called first shook the stadium. I heard Mrs. Crabtree say, "Hot Dog!" Then I saw her leap through the gate. Tinsley gave a hoot and ran in the arena after her, and then I heard DJ yell, "Way to go, Annie!" I left the lineup for my ribbon and trophy. The real triumph was having a first great show experience for Shammy and for us as a team. The win was just a bonus, even in my un-tailored, old-fashioned suit.

# CHAPTER 16

## JOURNAL ENTRY: THE INVISIBLE HOUSE

HELLO DOLLIE WAS THE FIRST horse I learned how to do patterns with. After lessons here with Mrs. Crabtree, I am now assuming Dollie was like most beginner horses. Someone could whisper in her ear what pattern was to be expected, and she would go do it. Okay, not that easy, but she was willing. That being said, it was only possible because of the hard work of people like Anne and Tina. They worked their tails off teaching Dollie her patterns. I was five or six when I started riding in the 9 & Under classes in California, and they'd done most of the work to get me and Dollie ready, and I hadn't realized how much work that was.

Now I'm a Crabtree rider, and learning pattern work takes more practice and patience than I ever realized. And remembering to never ever leave my thinking cap in the dorm room or wherever. I love the fact that Mrs. Crabtree teaches us to train the horses to do pattern work. When she talks you through a lesson, she pretty much feels like she is riding with me. Being able to say I do lots of the work gives me a sense of pride and accomplishment when Shammy and I do a pattern right.

Diagraming a circle—like one might do in a math class—is easy on paper, but it takes a little time to process for riders on horses. Maybe because it involves six legs and two minds, and only one of the minds knows what is going on, or because the four legs drawing in the circle are at the mercy of the human on top of them. They have to trust the human to guide them around, to make a complete and round circle, and the horse still doesn't understand why they are doing this task. I had to make my body, my limbs, the key to communicate with Shammy, earning her trust with every move and signal I give her. With this trust, the ride becomes enjoyable. While riding, I have learned to never say, "It's easy." Once the trust is there, maybe instead of wanting to go hang out with the other horses in the lineup, Shammy wants to do these circles with me instead.

Mrs. Crabtree had several ways to show us how to execute a circle. She would tell us to make four imaginary marks at each quarter of the circle, and then ask, "If your horse needs sixteen strides to make the circle, how many strides are in each quarter?" To me, this sounded like a math problem rather than a riding lesson, but for some reason, the number was easy to figure out, and most of us proceeded to make our circles. Sometimes she would draw a circle on the glass in her booth with her finger, then cut the circle once in half and one more line across, making four equal slices. A light would go off as a sudden four popped into our heads. It takes four strides to get to each of your imaginary quarters while aiming for the next imaginary quarter mark and then the half way mark, turning all the while. Out loud, we counted loud enough that she could hear us in the booth, or until she knew we were counting automatically. If a horse needed twenty strides, or even if they didn't need it but the rider somehow didn't reach the first mark until stride five, a sudden math correction or making the turn slightly tighter on the back end would need to be made by the rider, or your circle wouldn't come out even. We were kept on our toes and taught to think quick. With a twenty-stride circle, we would need more of the ring but can't use the rail because it will cause a straight line. Today's circle was part of a pattern she had made up for us, which was: Trot down the rail on the correct diagonal. Stop. Execute a canter circle. Stop. Drop your stirrups. Reverse. Canter on the incorrect lead halfway down the rail, transition into the trot, halt. Pick up your irons—stirrups—and walk to the lineup. Patterns like these make my day. I like change in routines, and I love challenges. Trying to make patterns perfect is a challenge. On the day you think this is going to be easy, that is the day it will be the hardest.

A figure eight is not a snowman, nor is it the infinity sign. It's an eight. Two circles that happen to be touching. We picture it in our heads; we draw the figure eight out with our eyes in the arena, marking the spots on the walls and in the dirt. Then we are asked to execute a figure eight. Applying leg aids is kind of like squeezing a ginormous tube of toothpaste with your legs. We have to guide our horses around the circle not only by squeezing our legs but by applying our hands as well. This is done by lowering the circle's inside hand down, almost as if the hand is pulling them around the circle, but without exaggerating the movement. It's a slight lowering of the hand with a shorter rein length. At the same time, I have to count strides and watch for the imaginary marks. It's also important to think ahead because my horse is always thinking of the horses in the lineup or being in their stall. There is nothing convincing them to be working in the middle of the arena while their friends are standing together on the other end of the arena.

No matter what the distraction, a round circle can be the hardest thing in the world to do on horseback. Mrs. Crabtree has a thousand ways to describe how it should be done and how you are doing it wrong. Today, my figure eight somehow became a lesson with me riding my horse through and around both sides of a house. Mrs. Crabtree said things like, "You must go out the front door, start turning gradually, and don't enter the house again until you are in the back yard. When you come around and can face the back door, go inside. Stop in the middle of the house. For the next circle, we must go out the front door and wait to get off the front steps before turning. Make your turn in the front yard, go around the house, and when you are in the back yard behind the house, then enter in the back door." This house was becoming part of my daytime nightmare. Something good was in the kitchen because Shammy took a shortcut back into the house through the bathroom window, and I let her. The next figure eight was better, but we never ended on only one good figure eight.

The next one, my leg aids failed us again, and Shammy went into the "window" and ended up cantering through the "den." It didn't end there though. We even left the house early and ended up going through the window of the front room. It wasn't a good day for this imaginary house—I'd made a mess of it. It seemed like Shammy and I did fifty figure eights until we executed two correct figure eights in a row. Not everything is easy. I thought a simple figure eight should have been a piece of cake or pie. At least now, I think I am ready for the unexpected, and maybe it will be easier to handle or fix the next time we need to canter or trot around and through the house. One thing about this lesson is that it has been forever embedded in my head. You would have thought I would have learned my lesson on bringing a horse into a house with my experience with Vicky. Apparently not!

Learning patterns is a slow process. It's like training for a marathon rather than going for a stroll. Shammy and I needed to learn them quickly, but we couldn't learn everything in a day, not even two. We learned enough to get by at a show, then we would come home, and Mrs. Crabtree would teach us more to make them perfect. She describes *a serpentine* as a series of half oranges. If you were not hungry before your lesson, you would be hungry after your lesson. I've had a few lessons working on serpentines, and I never want to see another orange again. After describing the pattern she was asking for, it was up to us—the riders—to figure out all the details like what way to start it, what way to be facing when I end the serpentine, and how many loops—sorry, half-circles—are needed. Then we are asked to execute these, and sometimes she wouldn't comment until everyone was finished to see if we simply followed the first person's pattern or did something different. Always thinking! Dollie and I had done several serpentine's for judges in classes in California, and I even did some on High Hopes, but making the half-circles similar and fit within the ends of the arena was more the goal than counting to make sure they were a specific number of strides. Mrs. Crabtree demanded perfection. Unless a judge asks for a serpentine to be done a specific direction, they are left up to the rider, so once we chose how or what direction we were going to execute our serpentine, I would have to find the marks and spots on the walls, hoping they were correct. The other huge thing was not to forget to count my horse's strides—outload—and make sure the half-circles had all the same number of strides. No straight lines, except for that one stride across the adjoining half-circle—that must be exactly at right angles to the line—and the arch only to the next circle. Every rider heard this explained again and again as they worked on their serpentine. As for myself, I heard it again in my sleep, and I am sure Shammy dreamt of doing them as well.

As the serpentine lessons went on, we had so many orange halves that some of us girls would have liked to toss a lemon half and several grapefruit halves in the mix. It was during our serpentine lessons that I missed California the most. I missed our fruit trees that were between the barn and the house, and I missed Chino's vegetable shop. But back to Kentucky.

I was beginning to feel pride as Shammy bent around the half-circles. My voice commands were starting to be understood, my leg aids and hands were engaged, and I'd found my spots. The transitions were smooth, my numbers matched, and we ended it with a halt and a big deep breath. Pride stands for "Practice, Repetition is Devine Equitation." I just made that up. It was the best feeling to have completed the perfect serpentine with my teammate, Shammy, but now I'm hungry for citrus and missing California.

Imaginary lines were visualized everywhere in the arena as we worked. *A straight line* is a straight line, no matter where it is drawn. It's a straight line, no matter if it's from three feet off the rail down to the end of the arena, or diagonally across the arena from end to end, or slicing the arena down the middle, or in the middle going either direction. Visualizing it is a piece of cake. Executing it can be entertaining for everyone involved, except maybe for Mrs. Crabtree.

Following an imaginary straight line means a rider has to be able to hold their horse's body straight on the same line. No fishtailing and no weaving or side passes of any kind should happen. This is the one time your mind is thinking, *I only have to point my horse to the marked spot and go there.* The funniest thing about that thought is your horse didn't understand the assignment, and she has other thoughts—like maybe circles—in mind. One of their favorite thoughts is that they have really decided they like the comfort of the rail. It's a habit, a routine. Before you know it, your horse will slowly drift to it, and you find yourself on the rail. Another is because you typically ask for a canter-lead and make a circle, they begin to guess or assume what way to turn because of the lead you asked them to take. I guess that's why we are asked to take the incorrect lead and make a circle once in a while.

But with a straight line, after so many failed attempts, the two-hundred-foot arena starts to feel like it's two hundred yards long, and the end is unreachable. The moment you get the line perfect, you suddenly ask yourself, *Why was that so hard?*

Mrs. Crabtree makes sure we have our "thinking caps on" every moment of every ride, and come to think of it, she asks us to always think inside and outside of the arena.

*Sketch by Helen K. Crabtree 1938-39*

# CHAPTER 17

## JOURNAL ENTRY: JUST ONE OF THE GIRLS

RUNNING PATTERNS ON FOOT BEFORE our equitation class is a requirement for every one of us Crabtree equitation riders. Outside, we line up on foot and pretend we are on our horses. One of us steps out of the line and executes the posted pattern. We could easily show left and right leads with our feet, but we raise our hand to indicate which diagonal we are posting. As we do this, each step we take is to be counted, just as it is to be done on our horses. Lines are straight, circles are round, and intersections for changes or stops are made on the marks. This helps us remember the workout, picturing it in our heads and moving through the motions. We had already been to the arena and marked our stops and sections there, and now we are running through the pattern to confirm it is in our heads. Each time one of the other riders has a turn, we watch, count and memorize.

Most of the older riders look bored out of their minds running through patterns on the ground, but for some reason, I think it's the coolest thing. Maybe because I am a new Crabtree Girl, but this definitely sets us apart from all the other barns. Mrs. Crabtree seems to have the best teaching tricks. I realized how blessed I am that I can ride with her. It's hard work, but sometimes it's nice to not think, so this afternoon, I am going to the pool with all the Crabtree riders simply to float in the pool and chill.

# CHAPTER 18

## JOURNAL ENTRY: DREAMING OF PONIES

L EXINGTON IS CONSIDERED THE SECOND largest American Saddlebred horse show of the season, sort of the warm-up for Louisville. It's held on a racehorse track like the Cincinnati horse show. There are so many beautiful horses showing, and if I wasn't in a class riding at the horse show, I was in the Crabtree box, watching the show. If there weren't enough seats, I was somewhere close, in the stands or on the rail.

Everything amazed me. In California, there wasn't a pony five-gaited class. The classes were open to all size horses, even those under fourteen hands and two inches, which are considered ponies. This would have been the class where Hercules would show. Boy, did this class look like fun! At the shows, the crowd goes wild when the announcer says, "Rack on." The 17 & Under five-gaited pony championship was in the arena, and goosebumps raised my arm hairs straight up. It was exciting, but something tugged at my heart. It made me miss riding

Hercules. I also started to realize he was our "bicycle with training wheels" for learning how to ride a gaited horse.

As I watched the five-gaited pony class here at Lexington, I could only imagine what I must have looked like out in the show ring in California with Hercules. We must have zig-zagged around that arena so much there was no way the judges could have missed us. They were probably amazed at the little peanut staying on. I bet the judges watched to make sure I had control. Showing against all those big five-gaited horses with my spotted pony. But never underestimate Hercules. He could sometimes out rack all of them. He was so much fun to ride and show.

Here at Crabtree's, I am learning that spacing, rail placement, when to move, and where to go are all a part of a strategy of making you and your horse look your best. However, Hercules and Anne already taught me some of these tricks to stay alone, to pass, and not to get covered up. Hercules and I needed our space on the rail, so we would maneuver by passing other horses without turning too quickly to entangle his fast-moving legs. It was easy to get stuck behind another horse on the rail, but when Anne told me horses sometimes get kicked that way, I never again got close to the back end of another horse. I didn't realize how much he and Anne had taught me at such a young age, at least not until now. I was taught because a wrong move would have been a fast-moving disaster, which is why spacing is necessary in the show ring.

It also made me happy to think of how many people I know that Hercules taught. He was a training machine with magical powers that could transform kids from passengers to riders. I, too, "out-grew" him, although not in size. I was ready for a nicer show horse, and Hercules was passed on to one of DJ's friends in California, Jimmy Cherry. He rode the socks off that Paint Pony. Everyone had a blast learning the five gaits that the American Saddlebred horse can do on Hercules.

Today, I sat there in the Crabtree box, along the rail at the Lexington horse show, dreaming what it would be like to show my own five-gaited pony here in Kentucky with Crabtree Farms.

## JOURNAL ENTRY: FEELING THE UNDEFEATED PRESSURE

THE ICE-COLD AIR-CONDITIONED BREEZE ESCAP-ING the building hit my face as I walked into the Freedom Hall Arena in Louisville, Kentucky. The familiar bright green shavings topping several feet of deep soil laid out the footing for the horses. As I looked at the green shavings being outlined with the freshly painted white fence railing, goosebumps appeared up and down my arms. In the center of this huge arena, outlined in bright gold mum flower planters, was a square sitting area for the judges, announcer, show secretary, and ringmaster. Five-Gaited World's Grand Champion names hung on the walls the entire perimeter between the first section of seats and the upper seats, displaying the first winner in 1902 to last year's winner. The chills were not from the air conditioner. I felt my heart beating a little faster than normal as I took in the sight. No horses were in the arena yet. Mrs. Crabtree expected all of her riders to go look at the arena, study it, and then come back to the stable area and get ready to ride.

Shammy felt my nerves as she put her ears back when I first sat down on her. Tinsley must have seen something too, and he popped me on the leg with the back of his hand, telling me, "Snap out of it. It's just another horse show." I couldn't get it out of my head that I have been undefeated on Shammy in this class all year. What if I blow it here? What if I freeze like I did last year on High Hopes? We followed Tinsley to the warm-up arena. The classes were huge, but I knew I had a target on my back. I was the one to beat! Strange, last year, no one knew my name, and this year, a different story. I wasn't the new Crabtree girl any longer. Shammy and I were quite the team, but this was our first world's championship together.

Dad must have known how to slap me out of the state I was in. He came over and said, "Win this class, and we will buy you a three-gaited or five-gaited pony."

What! More pressure, but this statement made me forget about the green shavings and where we were. I'd been challenged. I gulped the hot, muggy August air and concentrated on breathing until Shammy's ears went forward, telling me she was relaxed and happy.

An odd feeling rushed over me, remembering how I learned how to canter Fame in order to get my own pony, Vicky. They hadn't thought I would canter Fame that quickly, but Dad knew I would do it. In the lineup, I didn't see my dad and couldn't find him anywhere. He wasn't sitting with Mom. When I made my victory pass, he met Shammy and I leaving the arena. Later, he told me he had to hide in the bathroom because he was so nervous for me. Mom and Dad purchased the World's Champion Three-Gaited Pony, Chablis Premier, from Mr.

Tom Moore. One of his daughters rode him in the championship, and I couldn't believe he was going to be mine. My only hesitation is that he is a world's champion, so the pressure for me to win with him next year was going to be huge. I guess this is another challenge I am definitely up for!

The whole show was surreal. The excitement was indescribable, but all I could dream about was next year. Like a little kid riding for the first time and then begging for more by saying, "Again, again!"

# CHAPTER 20

## JOURNAL ENTRY: GIRL SAILING

IT WAS A SUMMER TO always remember where dreams did come true. I hadn't thought it was possible to love riding and showing more than I already did, but I do. Although I was sad to leave Shammy and Split Second in Kentucky, I couldn't wait to get back to California. It took HoneyBear almost a full day until she would "speak" to me, but once we went to bed, she jumped in bed and curled up with me like she did four months ago.

School is supposed to start tomorrow, but I won't be seeing any of my friends because we are moving…sort of moving. I guess when Mom and Dad told me we were going to live on a boat, I didn't believe them. I can't bear the thought of leaving HoneyBear or Vicky for almost a year. Things are happening so fast, but slow. I know this doesn't make sense because it doesn't make sense to me either.

It was a year ago that Mom and I first went to Kentucky to ride with Mrs. Crabtree as guest riders. A short time after that, Mom got sick and ended up in the hospital. Dad had to take me to show in the CPHA finals. Anne took Dollie for me to ride instead of High Hopes because he had just arrived back from Kentucky. It was amazing that I won the 17 & Under CPHA finals at age 10. I am the youngest rider to ever win it! But with Mom in the hospital, it seemed unreal, like it didn't happen. Then the whole year seemed to flash past me. Mom was feeling better when DJ and I flew off to Kentucky, and she came to visit us a few times and watched us show, but now we are packing for our trip to the Atlantic Ocean on the *Western Star*. I don't want to leave California.

This is crazy. Will all the things Mrs. Crabtree taught me be lost? We only have one more show before we leave, and we are flying out to Kansas City and then off to The Bahamas.

I am going to the barn. I must go hug Vicky.

# CHAPTER 21



MY BODY FELT WEAK, NEARLY paralyzed, with a mix of heartbreak, frustration, and anger. These feelings swirled inside my veins as Shammy and I left the show arena. Mrs. Crabtree was angry, and it sure felt like she was angry at me because after being undefeated the whole show season, I was beat here in Kansas City in the UPHA finals. It would be a whole other year before competing for the UPHA Challenge Cup 14 & Under championship again.

Another full year!

We were the first out of the arena as reserve champions. I looked around for Tinsley, but another Crabtree groom quickly arrived to escort us through the warm-up area, back to the stables. Tinsley was wiping down Bell Hop, preparing him for DJ's class that was going in next. DJ looked shocked seeing me and asked what happened. I could only shake my head and hold back tears. I wasn't going to be a bad sport, but I found it hard to speak to

DJ. Then my emotions almost got the best of me when I heard Tinsley scold me. "Aaat, yo better get that out of your head before Mrs. Crabtree sees ya." I shook my head and wished DJ luck, adding, "Have fun!" Bell Hop was as tall as Shammy, but his neck was much longer and set higher. Bell Hop was fresh, ready for his class, and held his head high, which added to the length of his neck. Tinsley continued to rub him with his towel, giving DJ and Bell Hop a last-minute rest before their class. They looked like champions. Maybe today, they will take that blue streak away from the undefeated team. DJ was the undefeated reserve champion most of the season, and they were ready for a blue ribbon and victory pass.

My plan was to walk Shammy back to the barn and come back to the show ring for his class, but Mrs. Crabtree pulled me into the tack room. My blood seemed to drop from the upper part of my body, and for a brief minute, I thought the world spun a little faster and hoped I wouldn't fall down. I tried not "showing" my bad sportsmanship but feared this was going to be that lesson. Instead, she wrapped her arms around me and hugged me. My shoulders dropped. The spinning inside me subsided. I wasn't alone. She held me, and all I wanted to do was cry, but I suddenly felt more love than anger. She assured me that we had a great ride and did everything right. The win could have gone either way, and today wasn't the day. It was amazing to feel her love this strong, and with her help, I suddenly felt stronger for it—still heartbroken, but stronger.

She put her hands on my shoulders, looked into my eyes, and grinned, then slipped out the door. My mind no longer raced. Since I was in the changing room, I put my gloves and whip away and hung my jacket, then went to Shammy's stall to show her love before heading to the arena for DJ's class, which I heard had already reversed directions. I started to jog down the long aisle, but I knew to stop because other horses—being pulled out of stables and onto the concrete aisle way—shouldn't get spooked by my running. I walked as fast as my little legs could carry me though. The paddock announcer once again updated the barns on the progress of the class and made the final announcement for the next class. Another disappointing feeling rushed over me. I missed DJ's ride. When I arrived at the warm-up arena, another Crabtree groom grabbed me and simply said, "You have to go back to the barn." My mind was swimming from the gasps people were making and trainers getting off their horses to run toward the show ring. The paddock announcer called for the horse show veterinarian, and an ambulance appeared. Then suddenly, I was back at our stalls, my mind still swirling.

Trainers, grooms, riders, and horses seemed to be in a fog, unable to process what was going on. I was told to stay, so I did. I listened to the whispers—the bits and pieces of conversations—and gathered these words: someone fell, slipped, and could die. So, the sight of DJ walking down the hall with our parents was the best thing in the world to me at that moment. Mom and Dad were walking close, almost as if shielding him from all the people trying to speak to him. He walked up to me and tearfully said, "They are going to kill him."

What! Without another word, my heart broke. The

words I was overhearing were coming together like a fog lifting to reveal a danger sign; a nightmare unfolding. Bell Hop had slipped trotting out of the arena, breaking at least one leg. After rushing Bell Hop to a horse hospital and taking X-rays, they found the break was too severe, and he would never be able to stand because his leg wouldn't be able to hold him up again. The ambulance called was for DJ, but after they checked him out, he was physically fine and released. We didn't know until a few hours later, but DJ must have known how bad Bell Hop's leg looked. Bell Hop was the first horse DJ really loved and loved to ride, and there I sat, helpless. Mom, Dad, and I stood with DJ while every trainer, exhibitor, groom, and even show ground personnel came to offer their sympathy to DJ.

After that class—that disaster—no horse show will be allowed to use plywood to make a ramp with only shavings on top. The rule doesn't have an official name, but every time I ride up and down a ramp, I will think of Bell Hop. Every time a horse enters and exits a show ring, it will be Bell Hop's rule that keeps them safe from slipping and falling.

JOURNAL ENTRY: OFF BALANCE

L IVING ON THE *WESTERN STAR* for the last nine months has been an experience! It is so good to be back with my horses, though I still miss HoneyBear and Vicky like crazy. They are in California, but Mom and Dad said they are going to purchase a farm in Kentucky so we can move here now that we spend all of our time here. Tinsley noted that I turned blonde and my skin was almost as dark as his, and we laughed together. It's so good to be back at Crabtree Farms. Shammy seemed to miss me too, or at least the sugar treats I sneak to her in her stall and our Shammy hugs.

DJ's new horse is named *Swiss Kiss*, and he calls him Swistifer. I can almost feel DJ's heartbreak over Bell Hop. Swiss Kiss is an elegant chestnut five-gaited gelding, but he's not Bell Hop. I am sad for DJ, but he should do well in his classes. Maybe that will help.

Chablis Premier, Chaby for short, is a blast to ride. He has all the power of a big horse stuffed into a little horse's body. I'm afraid I will be compared with Mr. Moore's daughter riding him. I know I will, but I will not look like her since I am almost a foot shorter than she is. I just hope I can show Chaby as well as she did! I've been riding him with Mrs. Crabtree. I guess I assumed Mr. Crabtree was going to train him since they just told me we have to retire Split Second. Over the winter, he hurt his foot, and they simply can't get him well enough to show again. If we sell him, it would be cruel for him to show in pain, so we decided to retire him. When Mom and Dad purchase a place here in Kentucky soon, Split Second will be hanging out with Dollie and Vicky!

It has been strange riding horses this week. At least we didn't have to wait for school to let out for summer before we could come back to Crabtree Farms. Doing school on the boat gave us some flexibility. We piled back into the girl's dormitory, most of us choosing to stay in our same rooms as last summer, and only a couple of the girls live close enough to drive here for their lessons. Today, it looks like most of us Crabtree girls who have arrived for the summer are having a lesson together.

A group of six Crabtree girls entered the arena for our lesson today—four was the norm, but six of us filed in on the rail. Rail spacing was more challenging, and rating our horse's speeds to make sure we were going about the same speed or pace as everyone in the arena was tricky. But it was fun having most of the girls in the arena at once. When I had a chance to look for spacing, I would watch the other older girls ride. I tried to sit and hold my hands like they were, trying to imitate their looks. Mrs. Crabtree must have seen my movements because she corrected me several times. To imitate doesn't always work, but they looked so perfect that I wanted to be like them. I needed to look taller, but this wasn't actually working, and today, I was feeling like a puppet. I need to find what works for me.

Mrs. Crabtree told us that our hands should look as if we are going to play a harp, and every movement of your fingers holding the reins should be soft, like the harpist plucking her instrument. At age eleven, I had never seen a harpist, so this wasn't going to be a good example, so then she went for the dancer example. Dancers look as if there is an invisible string connected to the top of their heads, gently pulling them up and stretching from the top of their heads through their necks, pulling every vertebra in their back upward, toward the ceiling. I took ballet when I was four, and then riding took over my life, and I never went back, but I remember the basics. I didn't think I was having issues with sitting up straight or how I held my hands until now. I feel I am being compared to all the Crabtree riders and will never look as good. I'm too short. They are tall, slender, and built like Mrs. Crabtree. How can I compete?

As we walked, we stretched, feeling the lift from the magical string in the center of our heads, pulling us upward through our neck vertebras, and all the way down to include the tailbone. If we started to arch, she would quickly correct us. "It's a pull straight upward, not backward." The only part of our bodies that should feel being pulled down and back are your shoulders, and we should feel our shoulder blades engage. "Keep that stretch," she instructed. "Now, start with both heels and stretch downward. Feel the pull all the way up through your calves, thighs, hips, and to your gluteus maximus."

As we continued to walk, stretching our upper bodies up to the ceiling of the arena and our heels and legs pulled downward, she asked us to halt. Mrs. Crabtree's instructions continued, "Drop your reins and place your hands on your thighs."

I started thinking back to when Anne Speck used to put our horses on a lunge line. While following her commands, we would trot in circles. It was like the Simon Says game, and I would ride without reins, reaching to the sky and out to the sides, helping us feel and be balanced. But this wasn't going to be anything like a Simon Says game, except that we were following her directions. She asked us to bend our elbows and gently fold our fingers together. We repeated this a couple times, and she asked if our hands were in the same position and same spot every time. We were asked to make a mental note of how our hands looked and where they were placed before addressing our reins and then continued the lesson. After placing these invisible strings in my head and my heels, maybe I *was* a puppet! Maybe Mrs. Crabtree was teaching me to be my own person. After all, Pinocchio ended up being a boy.

When practicing, we never know what Mrs. Crabtree is going to ask, and nothing she does ever gets boring to a rider or a horse. Today she asked us to reverse and canter. Not reverse and walk and then canter when you are ready. Nope, never would that be okay. This test was simple but never taken for granted. All aids need to be applied and done perfectly.

Everyone in the arena stopped their horses at the same time, and we all took a breath. It was if we were riding as one. Mrs. Crabtree asked us to look at our hands and compare them with the way they looked after the exercise we did earlier. Ah, it was starting to come to me. Mrs. Crabtree said to ride with 90% brains and 10% muscle, and she was training brains to make sure our hands were "thinking" correctly. Weird, but true.

In a lesson with all these beautiful horses and riders, it's hard to not compare myself. They make everything look easy. Their horses are so talented. They are perfection. Looking across the arena at each pair, I hope Shammy and I look half as good as they do. It's so hard not to compare myself with the other girls, especially when a judge does that for us at the horse shows. I have so much to learn, so much to retain, that my mind can't think of how they look. I must work on us—me and Shammy. I feel out of sorts, and it's almost as if Shammy is angry I went missing for so long. Plus, my legs are weak. They feel like jelly. I wish Vicky was here so I could ride all day to get my balance and legs back in shape.

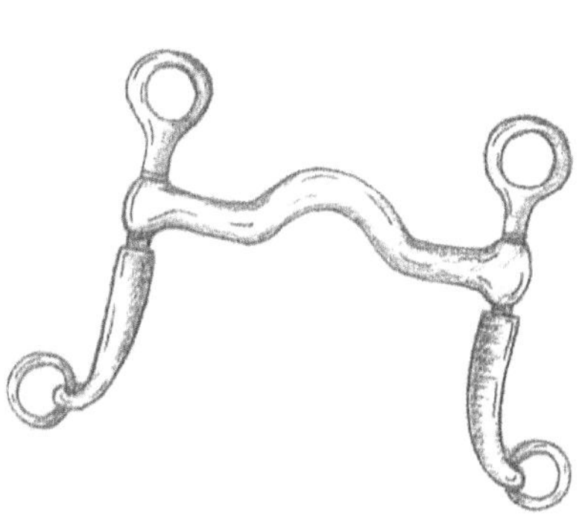

# CHAPTER 23

JOURNAL ENTRY: A POOF AT ROCK CREEK HORSE SHOW

WITH EACH RIDING LESSON, I learn something new. After riding Shammy for over a year, I thought things would become repetitious and even, dare I say, boring. When I arrived here as a new Crabtree rider, I didn't understand the importance of voice commands beyond a "Whoa!" for a stop, a cluck and leg pressure, or a slight hand movement forward—aiding her to go forward—because that's what I did in California. Mrs. Crabtree doesn't simply tell us to do something. She explains why she is asking us to do it that way. While doing patterns, these voice commands have proven their importance. Shammy still gets nervous during our pattern work, but I have learned to talk to her, hold my hands still, and the whip that I must carry is unnoticed. Typically, if I breathe and stay relaxed, she does as well. She has more confidence about our next move, our transition, when she hears my voice saying "Walk" or "Trot" and carries her ears ahead, looking forward to the next command.

If Shammy anticipates the canter, this could be tragic

because—being nervous, out of position, or leading with the leg you need—she is sure to take the wrong lead. Each step of a pattern is done during practice at Crabtree's, and we sometimes do them in sections to relax her. We might give an extra minute in between, stopping her to give her a pat on the neck and praise her when she is doing well. I can feel Shammy before she is going to mess up. I can feel her anticipate the incorrect lead. The trick is to wait for the other shoulder to lead before allowing her to move forward. It's a mix of feeling her body, watching her ears, and feeling the bits in her mouth. I not only can picture our pattern shapes and mark our points or intersections, but I can see what she is physically seeing and anticipate her reactions. Mrs. Crabtree trains us to train our horses, and it's empowering when you and your horse do everything right. This doesn't happen all the time—sometimes only once a month—but when it happens, it's special.

All the work we do at Crabtree's can seem to go unnoticed at the show at times. Mrs. Crabtree warns us by telling us what has happened to others in the past. It's a history lesson worth knowing so as not to make the same mistakes as those we follow. She covers the what-ifs during most of our lessons by telling us real stories that sometimes are so crazy they are hard to believe. But I am learning how to deal with situations that arrive unexpectedly. However, nothing could have prepared me for what happened during the Rock Creek UPHA challenge cup class on Shammy.

The class had lined up, waiting to execute our individual workouts; our patterns. When my number was called, Shammy and I began. After we were about to complete the first half-circle of a serpentine, a stride away from stopping, an explosion of baby powder erupted in the air in front of us. Streaks of white powder shot up about fifteen to twenty feet high. After the baby powder peaked, it slowly floated downward like a showering blanket of fluff. Even though I couldn't see Shammy's face, I could sense that her eyes were bugged out, and her nose was flared. She snorted, almost like a human says, "Humph." All four of her legs had frozen stiff underneath me. She wasn't going forward for anything or anyone.

We had a couple more half-circles to complete this serpentine pattern before transitioning into the left lead to complete the next half-circle, but with her legs locked straight, her mind definitely wasn't on me anymore. I could feel her thoughts. Yes, her thoughts. She wanted to spin around and run away from the explosion of white powder.

I anticipated her spinning on her haunches and fleeing from the scene, but I was able to keep her still, frozen, and she didn't dart off. I held my reins firm without pulling her back, keeping a firm grip with both my legs. I spoke to her with a gentle but firm voice, "Whoa, Shammy. Easy. Easy, girl." I simply asked her to stand. The scary white powder floated toward the ground, which felt like a ten-minute ordeal. When it was all gone, I felt her take a breath. She had no idea where we were or what we were doing. This baby powder bomb had erased all her thoughts. There wasn't a plan, so I reacted the only way I knew how to react. Calmly, I spoke to her until I had her attention again. Her ears relaxed, and I could feel her muscles release the tense bulges underneath me. I shortened my reins as if we were going to walk, and I actually told her to walk because I needed her to take the first step to unlock her legs. On the second step, when her left leg was in position, I softly gave her my leg aid and asked her to canter. Guiding her with every aide taught to me, we completed the next half-circle and then stopped. I waited a few seconds before asking her to do anything, then slowly squeezed my left leg in and aided her for the right lead. "Easy girl," I said, and we completed the serpentine. I patted her and told her she was a good girl. Shortening my reins again, I trotted back to the lineup, where I thought I should just leave the class.

My thoughts were filled with what had just happened. I was proud of Shammy for not spinning around or jumping away. I was also proud of her for finally relaxing and coming back to me. I know her mind was blown by that "white stuff" she had never seen before. As we stood in the lineup, I wondered who did that and why, but my biggest concern was Shammy. A voice came over the loudspeaker, and instead of the announcer, it was the judge. She said she felt compelled to say something, not only about the safety concerns of what had happened during this class, but that one of the reasons she was giving the first place blue ribbon to this rider was because she outthought the person who was responsible for the explosion of powder. I started to cry. I knew she was talking about me and was never so thankful that I had Mrs. Crabtree as my trainer. She had taught me to be present, focused on the moment, use my brains, and do what is right for that horse. I didn't let anyone blow my horses mind. I kept her feeling safe, and she trusted me.

Later, Mrs. Crabtree said, "You saved your horse for the rest of the show season, and possibly for the rest of her equitation career."

I felt a lump build in my throat, and the only thing I wanted to do was give Shammy a hug. Each lesson, I learn something new. If you are present in everything you do, you may or may not be rewarded for it, but I was proud of this blue ribbon because it gave me strength over a bully trying to sabotage my ride!

## CHAPTER 24

JOURNAL ENTRY: TIME TO EVACUATE

THERE WERE SEVERAL REASONS WE didn't have many individual lessons. Probably the biggest reason is that there are so many of us riders, there wouldn't be enough time in the day. When I first arrived, Shammy and I had lessons alone, but I had to ride before dawn. So, for our group lessons, Mrs. Crabtree chose which students would be riding together and what time the lessons would be. Most of the time, the students not riding would be assigned to watch the others' group lessons from the teaching booth. As I walked up the steps and into the enclosed booth, Mrs. Crabtree patted the chair next to her, inviting me to sit as she began instructions for those in the arena. She spoke clearly into the microphone that was placed on a little desk-like shelf in front of her seat and simply said, "Walk." As she watched intensely, the riders walked around the arena, poised and proper, and every rider on their mounts looked like paired perfection.

Placement and spacing while riding is a big deal during lessons and in the show ring. Learning when to pass, when to circle at the end of the arena, or cutting across the arena—whatever is necessary to work by yourself—was an everyday lesson, even at the walk. At this point, I wasn't sure what Mrs. Crabtree's most important lesson was, but with all of her lessons, she embedded even the smallest details into our heads. Lessons we learned were how to enter the arena, how to sit in the saddle with proper legs, arms, and hands placement, looking alert, how to ride your horse into the corners, how to place yourself, and how to be aware of the other horses in the arena. Absolutely everything was important, and she told us why. When she taught, it felt like she was explaining things in three or four different languages. If you didn't understand her explanation one way, she said it another way so you could understand. It was interesting to listen to because she told stories about past riders and horses she would use as examples.

As I watched the lesson, anyone could tell by how they sat in the saddle that they were elegant and beautiful riders and horses; how each pair matched one another physically and mentally. They were working as if they were in a show ring being judged, looking their best even at practice. These were top-notch riders, and Mrs. Crabtree expected their very best every second of every ride.

As the other four of us riders sat in the booth watching the lesson in the arena, Mrs. Crabtree's Bull Dog, Ben, went from sitting under her legs to bucking up against our chairs if to say, "Move!" He plopped himself under and around the legs of our chairs. He wiggled and grunted until he was comfortable, and when our attention was back on the riders in the arena, Ben began to snooze, then he started to snore, and his snoring became obnoxiously loud. Typically, Mrs. Crabtree reaches down with her long, slender arm and rubs his head gently. Ben cracks one eye open to give her a glance and stops snoring, adjusts his body, and closes his eyes, once again asleep. However, this time she couldn't reach him, so she stomped the plywood floor to wake him. His one eye opened, and he grunted as if to say, "What!" With his opened eye, he looked at every one of us girls in total disgust. *How dare you wake me,* he must have thought. He then wiggled around to make himself more comfortable.

We continued watching the lesson. Then someone gasped behind me, and the next girl did the same. A moment later, I gagged and quickly held my breath to not puke. Panic raced through our heads, our bodies frozen in time, waiting and hoping Mrs. Crabtree would soon notice before we passed out. The other girls and I couldn't run out or laugh. We simply started to turn green. Ben had passed a SBD—silent but deadly. He'd farted. Mrs. Crabtree dropped the microphone, making a loud and crashing pop, and a bang rang out from the speakers in the arena as she suddenly jumped out of her chair, knocking it over. She let out a loud, ghastly shriek. "Beeeennnnnn!"

We couldn't seem to move fast enough. Chairs were flying everywhere. We practically ran over one another, trying to escape the teaching booth to reach fresh air. Mrs. Crabtree began waving her notebook frantically above Ben, fanning the stench from the booth toward the door. With no avail, she soon had to evacuate the booth. Running down the six steps, Mrs. Crabtree yelled, "Walk!" to the girls on horses and joined us. She bent over, gasping for fresh air. Tears began to stream down our cheeks as we tried holding ourselves up and not fall on the dirt barn aisle because we were laughing too hard.

Ben had exited the booth and walked up to all of us, standing between the arena and the barn aisle. He stared at us with a dazed looked, turned his nose up at us as though we were rude for waking him up from his nap, spun on his haunches, and headed down the barn aisle in search of Mr. Crabtree. Mrs. Crabtree was laughing so hard, I wasn't sure how she was able to keep from falling on the ground. This made us girls laugh even harder. She held her hands on her head, and all of us thought her wig was going to come off. After we wiped our tears and caught our breath, Mrs. Crabtree motioned for us to go back into the booth. Luckily, Ben's smell was no longer lingering there. We went back into the small teaching booth, but no one closed the door for a long while.

That was not what we were expecting to learn today. I actually can't remember today's lessons. Maybe it was to bring a gas mask into the teaching booth next time. Oh, Ben.

## JOURNAL ENTRY: A PERFECT TEN

AFTER WORKING ON THE RAIL, the four of us riders lined up at the end of the arena near Mrs. Crabtree's teaching booth, facing the middle of the arena, ready for our tests. Tests, or "patterns," as they were called on this end of the country, were called workouts back in California. We lined up as we always do, looking as if we were being judged at every second. When we were told which one of us would go first and what test we would do, the others sat and watched. While watching the other riders perform their patterns, we were required to sit up without slouching, hands up in position, heels down, looking directly ahead of our horses. We sat and watched as if we were in a class in full attention, and boy, did my arms hurt from being in that position for so long.

All horses and riders have good days and bad days working on patterns. Paula's horse is pretty green, which means he is new at pattern work. Mrs. Crabtree called for a sandwich figure eight. Food seems to always work its way into pattern work around here, but this sandwich is where the bread is represented with a trot circle, and the canter two circles are the meat or whatever is in your sandwich. A figure eight—one circle at the trot, the second and third at the canter, and the final circle again at the trot—thus sandwiches the canters between two trot circles. I said "simple," didn't I? Never, ever again will I say "simple" when it comes to any pattern work riding for Mrs. Crabtree. I have seen the tests, "back your horse," and even a "performance on the rail," which is a simple trot down and canter back—or whatever the judge requests. I've seen these tests repeated fifteen plus times to get it done the correct way. The "simpler" the workout or pattern, the more demanding Mrs. Crabtree is because it's expected to be executed perfectly. All of us Crabtree girls are expected to be perfect at home, so at the horse shows, patterns are performed for a judge with ease.

As we stood in the lineup, it was hard not to notice the jog cart that had been left inside the arena from a horse being worked before our lesson. It wasn't an odd thing. Sometimes they are left in the arena for the next horse. Mrs. Crabtree likes them removed, but this one seemed to be in a position that we could ride around the jog cart, making our figure eight circle. Jog carts are used to keep horses conditioned without putting a rider on their back every day. The horses are "jogged" by being hooked up with a harness and buggy—a two-wheeled jog cart—for exercise. So, Mrs. Crabtree told us to make the circle to the right, around the jog cart.

Paula shortened her reins, tapped her horse gently with the whip in order to get his attention, and moved out of the lineup, circling around behind the line to get the horse warmed up from standing. Then she trotted down to the three-quarter mark and stopped, pivoting her horse toward the center of the arena and the spot where she would be approaching her figure eight center mark. This was being executed perfectly. Her first loop was to the left, away from the end where we were standing, and the circle looked good, or at least it looked great from my angle. It was a classic out the front door, around the side of the house, and enter the house once again from the back door perfect circle, and she stopped her horse on the imaginary spot. Now, her right circle would be at a canter coming toward us, and for the horse, which is a herd animal, he will probably want to come back to his friends in the lineup. Plus, they will have the jog cart to canter around, and the worst that might happen is any horse might shy away from the cart, and the circle will be extra-large. My bet was that this was going to be Mrs. Crabtree's lesson today.

Paula kept her horse's body straight like she should, not to miss going out of the front door of the circle. She asked her horse for the right-lead to start making her circle around the jog cart, but *wham*! Her horse jumped sideways. Instead of jumping away from the cart, for no known reason, he was on top of the jog cart, kicking and stomping it to smithereens. Paula was left standing exactly where he jumped from, as if he'd vanished from underneath her. The three of us in the lineup held on as our horses spun around, trying to flee from this now-riderless horse that had somehow trapped himself inside a jog cart, who kicked it while it looked like he was bouncing on all four hooves. Crunching, banging, and loud thrashing sounds filled the arena as pieces of the jog cart went fly-ing. Paula stood near her figure eight's center mark with her hands out, saying, "Whoa!" Mrs. Crabtree left her as she and several grooms ran into the arena to help Paula's horse.

Shammy was snorting at the sight of this strange exhi-bition of a buggy demolition. Tinsley grabbed Shammy's reins and led us out of the arena at the same time the other two rider's grooms took them out.

I just saw a freak accident! Paula was totally fine, but her horse was, needless to say, spooked. After everything was good, except the poor jog cart, the grooms exited the arena with horse and rider in tow. In the barn aisle, the grooms told Paula that if a rider falls off, they have to buy the grooms a case of beer.

"Well, I would," she said, "but twelve-year-old kids can't buy beer." She had the best sense of humor of any rider—or person—I had ever known.

In California, DJ was in our arena at home practicing on his horse, Secret Call. The barns sat up on a hill at the end turn of the arena, and you could clearly see the space between the two barns. Someone up at the barn tossed a full bucket of water out just as DJ was coming around the end of the arena. Secret Call suddenly stopped at the sight of the mass of water in the air, and DJ flew into the air—over his horse's head and neck—doing a com-plete front flip and landing on his feet while still holding the reins. Everyone was completely frozen for what felt like five minutes in shock. DJ looked as if nothing had happened. Even the horse stood as if DJ was done with his lesson. I don't know if it was Anne, Mom, DJ, or someone else there watching, but cries of hysterical laughing erupted. "Ten!" someone shouted, which someone else repeated—a perfect score for DJ's dismount. Today's dismount seemed like another perfect ten for Paula. Her horse escaped injury—another ten. However, the jog cart wasn't that lucky. It looked like a pile of twigs from a tree with two random bicycle wheels lying there.

Today, I learned that a sense of humor can get someone through a tough ride. Laughter, especially around horses, can be the best medicine. I didn't truly understand this statement before today, but when I saw Paula laughing, it made me realize that as long as no one is hurt, laugh. It sure beats crying over something you can't control. Needless to say, the grooms all called her "Jog Cart" for the rest of the summer.

# CHAPTER 26

## JOURNAL ENTRY: OUR BLUE-GRASS HOME

THE SUN DANCES AROUND MY bedroom as it rises behind the barns outside my new room's window. Our new house is only minutes down the road from Crabtree Farms. Our barn has a few stalls for shade and for the horses to escape the crazy ice and summer storms that stir up frequently here in Kentucky. It's strange not living in the Crabtree dorms. I miss walking down to the barn and watching the horses work. I didn't realize how much I would miss living at Crabtree's, and especially Miss Hattie's cooking.

When I woke up this morning, HoneyBear was completely bothered as I pushed back the covers and crawled out from under her to leave the warmth of our bed. She lifted her head as if to say, "How dare you wake me." When I sat up and looked out the window, I saw Dollie, Split Second, and High Hopes all lined up at the fence, looking toward the house even though they have a field of green grass. They were waiting for their breakfast grain.

Even though my room is about a quarter size of my

bedroom in California, it's the best room in the house. Although the smallest, it has the best view of the barn and the horses. DJ has the whole basement to himself, and I hardly see him anymore. After Louisville, he told Mom and Dad he wanted a car, not a horse, and I was blessed with Swiss Kiss. They could have easily sold him because he is nice enough to always be in the top five in the 17 & Under juvenile five-gaited classes.

It's so different living in Kentucky, but I am truly blessed to be surrounded by all my horses. Vicky has the run of the small area in front of the equipment and hay barns, meaning less grass for her to founder on. Ponies eat the sweet, rich grass until they get sick. In California, we had dirt corrals and had to worry about horses eating dirt and clogging their intestines. A bran mash fed to them once a week helped it pass.

When I'm not at Crabtree's, I'm riding Dollie, Split Second, or High Hopes through the pastures and on the hills around the house and barns. Unlike California, Kentucky has fences all around the property borders, making it impossible to roam the hills and explore like I used to in California. It makes me miss California's open land, but being on a horse anywhere is the best feeling in the world. Trapped in field pastures beats not riding at all.

In California, I rode Vicky around the lima bean fields, strawberry fields, and into the eucalyptus "forest" following dirt roads for miles and miles. We explored Black Mountain and followed DJ's dirt bike paths, and on other days, we snuck off to the Del Mar beach areas. Hours were spent roaming Black Mountain, Rancho Santa Fe, and Del Mar. I can only imagine where I could have gone exploring on Dollie, Split Second, or High Hopes.

Lack of imagination gets you nowhere, so within the fence lines, I created games and spent hours making up patterns. While riding bareback using only a halter and no bridle, we performed each workout and pretended it was a new class offered at Louisville. Bareback equitation on retired horses only. In preparation for such a class, we must practice and practice some more. Oh, the obstacles I faced! While on Dollie, her magnetic force was driven by her boyfriend, High Hopes, who was happily back at the barn. She also found that not having a bit in her mouth gave me less control than normal and took full advantage of it. After completing the pattern, at least two perfectly executed in a row, we went back to the barn for her reward—getting back to High Hopes. I even made some patterns up for Split Second. We slow-gaited a couple large circles, claiming they were a figure eight, and I took it easy on him since he was a little tender-footed.

Wearing only a halter and lead rope, High Hopes held his head and neck as if he had his full bridle on with the curb and snaffle bit. His trot is becoming more like a shuffle, and he prefers his left lead, so for his sake, I create patterns just for him to perfect. Home is where I get dirty with my horses, covered from head to toe with their hair and dirt with every brush. Currying and brushing and rubbing them, I pamper them in their retirement years. The cold hose water trickling down my arm and into the pit of my arm was shockingly cold, reminding me to run cold water on their legs before washing their bodies. I pick their feet and comb their manes and tails. Spending time with them and taking care of them shows them how much I love them. They give back much more than unconditional love. They let me pamper them, but I know they love it because they both stand still near the fences or gates so I can climb on their back and go for a little ride.

# CHAPTER 27

## JOURNAL ENTRY: HOLD IT IN

GOOD HORSEMANSHIP IS GOOD SPORTSMANSHIP, and good riders shall always be good citizens. This is what Mrs. Crabtree enforces, and she expects nothing less of us. We are to be a good sport, no matter what happens. If you thought you should have won a class and expressed it in any way, she would say riding at Crabtree Farms might not be a good fit for you. You could go to the privacy of your own home and do what you want, but while at a show or at the barn at any time, while representing Crabtree Farms, that was clearly not the place. It wasn't something we, as Crabtree riders, picked up. Mr. and Mrs. Crabtree taught this to us not only in words but by example. This was taught to me early on with Anne and Royce as well, but at Crabtree Farms, the stakes were higher. I heard that some people were asked to leave the barn because of their behavior. I was glad I wasn't around for that!

Good horsemanship is not only a combination of excellence, competitiveness, mental excellence, and aggressiveness, it's also compassion. Mrs. Crabtree says, "Good riders should always be good citizens first." There is something about how she says things that makes me want to listen and follow her advice, and I always try.

Last week was Lexington Junior League, the "warm-up show" for Louisville. I am still thinking about the three-gaited championship class with Chablis Premier because of what happened. Not with the riders in the class, but with someone watching the class on the rail. I guess because Chablis Premier and I are "the ones to beat," coming into this year with my two back-to-back 17 & Under Three-Gaited Pony World's Championship titles, and three for Chablis. I get it. We have a target on our backs, but this only makes me want to defend our world's champion title more. Lexington's arena is a section of the racetrack in front of the grandstands at Lexington's Red Mile. We started trotting out of the narrow end, onto the straight-a-way, making another trip in front of two of the three judges. I was looking right at them and making sure another rider wasn't going to cut across the arena and cover me by placing their pony in between the judges and myself. Nor did I want to follow another pony too closely. Making a pass is very important to do alone.

As I was looking down the rail, I heard a whack. Chablis almost stopped in his tracks, tossing me forward onto his neck. Feeling him back down on his haunches, he felt like one of those quarter horses sliding to a stop. I reacted with a stern "Trot!" and a kick. Riding is an art of keeping a horse between you and the ground, but at this moment, I felt the ground rise up. Since he didn't fall, the next thing I anticipated he'd do was take off because something had scared him! I spoke to him, encouraged him, but he was doing more of a bunny hop. Apparently, the judges heard the noise, and trainers on the rail were yelling at someone, but I couldn't make anything out. My mind was focused on making Chablis trot while all three judges were looking right at us. After I felt he wasn't going to bolt, I was thinking it was his tail, so I looked back, but his tail seemed fine. A few moments later, he began to trot again as I spoke with him, trying to ease his fear.

As we headed toward the place in the arena again where it happened, Chablis slowed, and as expected, he tried to dart away. I noticed my father standing there as I rode past and heard him say something like, "It's okay, Annie. Just ride him." As we hit that same spot, Chablis didn't want to move forward, and a step later, he launched forward, but we stayed in the trot. Thank goodness the judges called for the shortest canter in history, and after, we quickly lined up. After the class, I noticed a line, a whelp, across Chablis's face. Someone had taken a whip and cracked it over his face! I wasn't told who it was but was promised, by my father, that it wouldn't happen again. Dad had seen it happen, and so had several other trainers, and they confronted the person. Dad told me he never left the person's side for the rest of the class. It wasn't losing the championship that bothered me—it was why someone would do that to an animal, and to me?

Good horsemanship is hard for me to understand right now. It's taking all of my energy not to scream. I want to know who it was and smack them down with a whip. There were several people standing around Dad when I saw him, so I wasn't sure exactly who it was that had assaulted my pony. Loving all animals has been who I am my whole life, so I don't understand this act of hate. My only revenge, though, will be to beat everyone at Louisville because that would mean also beating the person who took a whip to Chablis, an innocent animal. I don't know if Mr. or Mrs. Crabtree would approve of my feelings right now, but this assault was just that—an assault. I promised Chablis I would make it right, and I will try like mad to win the world's championship title again!

Today was my second lesson on him since the class at Lexington, and it was mind-blowing. I still can't shake my anger over someone hitting Chablis. The things he's doing only proves that he has a memory as good as an elephant. First, he doesn't know who hit him and simply no longer wants to trot down the rail. Every time we head out of the turn and toward the straight-away, he practically sits down on his haunches and does that same little bouncy thing, not wanting to move forward. He finally takes a few good steps, but not until we are toward the center of the ring. Mr. and Mrs. Crabtree were watching me ride from the middle of the arena, and the assistant trainer was standing at one end of the arena, with Tinsley at the other end. When I passed each one of them, they would start clapping their hands and making noise so he would move forward out of this strange squat-thing. Then we were told to trot again, and I made it around the corner to where he squatted, and Mrs. Crabtree banged the glass in her booth so hard that if Chablis didn't go, I was going without him. The loud banging scared the living daylights out of us both, but it seemed to work. Hopefully, we will have it all together for Louisville. It's only a week away. This ordeal is beyond upsetting. Inside, I want to cry, but outside, I am madder than a hornet at the person who did this to us.

The final ride before Louisville, and everyone took their places around the arena. Nothing scary, no fireworks, baby-powder, whips—besides my own…nothing crazy. Mrs. Crabtree had me hold my whip upward instead of down against his shoulder. I never question her theories or requests. I simply do what she tells me. Why would holding my whip up, upside down with the tip up in the air, help? If he thought about anything, I only had to shake it out to the side just slightly, and his attention was fully on me and not the people or anything else in the arena. I couldn't imagine how a whip would help since it was the cause of the problem, but for some reason, it worked. She said shake or move the whip so he can see it, so I did. Chablis kept his eye on the whip and his mind on me, and he never crouched or squatted again coming out of the corner. It wasn't what I did, but Mrs. Crabtree outsmarted this pony, and we were ready for Louisville.

I have a secret. I rode Chablis in the qualifying class but was not gunning for the win. I wanted to do well, but I rode him easy, against the rail. I wasn't going to let anyone cover me from the judges, but I wasn't going for it either. I was building his confidence in the arena, and maybe, I was building my own. We placed second, which would set us up to be in the championship, but not as the pony to beat. Maybe it would take the pressure off of us; make people forget about us. In the championship class, I entered the arena last, allowing everyone to make almost a trip around. We waited for the last call and entered just before they shut the gait. We trotted into the arena, cutting almost straight down the middle. Chablis had never been that close to the middle with all the flowers, chairs, and stuff in front of him, and this perked him right up. His ears where pinned forward, and he was snorting with excitement, exactly how an American Saddlebred was supposed to look. Every judge was looking at me, bordering on not knowing where I was going or knowing exactly what I was doing. I was going for the win. I was living on the edge!

After the first pass, I made it back toward the rail, making it clear that I was in charge of this ride. After the judges walked the lineup, I was a bit nervous. They didn't ask for a work-off, where they send their top riders back to the rail for a little extra. Not calling a work-off told me they'd made up their minds about who the winner will be. Normally, I'm the girl wearing the smile, always happy to be on a horse. In tonight's class, my cards were down on the table, and it was judgment time. I've never wanted to win so badly but couldn't do anything else. I sat there, not sure how it was going to end. I knew I did my best, but was it enough? More than the blue championship tri-colored ribbon, I wanted to see the person who wanted to beat me upset. Then I was really upset at myself for feeling this way.

When the announcer started introducing the sponsors of the class and everything, I missed the number they called. When no one made a move or left the lineup, it hit me. Then he said, "Your winner is Chablis Premier." Me!

Us! We won! When I noticed Mrs. Crabtree jogging out to the middle of the arena with Tinsley on her heels, tears streamed down my cheeks. I reached down with both arms and hugged Chablis, kissing him on his neck, then we made our way to the trophy presentation area as the crowd's cheers filled the stadium. They handed me at least two dozen red roses. Mrs. Crabtree put our championship tri-colored ribbon on Chablis's bridle. Tinsley helped hold him until he knew I had my reins organized. Chablis and I made our way down to the far end of the arena, where we waited for the other horses to exit before making our victory pass. I was trying to not drop the dozens of roses in my arms and reins in my hands while trying to control my very excited pony. I could hardly see through the tears swelling up in my eyes as we made our way down the rail for the very last time. Together, we were honored with three world's championship titles, making this Chablis's fourth WC in a row.

*Chief Beau-Champ*
*Sketch by Helen K. Crabtree*

# CHAPTER 28

JOURNAL ENTRY: MY HEART IN A KNOT SHOW-STOPPER

MY HEART SEEMS TO BE splitting in two. Although Shammy and I are working as one unit, obstacles seem to blow up in our faces. Her hugs after the classes are the only thing getting me through these crazy equitation classes. However, showing Swiss Kiss and Chaby is amazing, fun, and exciting. Swiss Kiss is the coolest five-gaited horse to show, not as fast as Split Second was, but a more elegant-moving horse. He and I hit it off very well. He is so much fun to ride, and the more I ask of him, the more he tries to give. While engaging my legs, tightening my leg grip around his sides—my seat firmly pressed down and back on the saddle—raising my hands, and slightly bumping his bits in his mouth as he began to slow-gait, it feels like we are gliding upwards; climbing stairs to the rafters. As I watch his head lifting, rising with every smooth step as he engages his back legs underneath us, it's how I would think Mr. Harris felt while riding his World's Grand Champion horse, Imperator.

Swiss Kiss loves the slow-gait. When I give the first

little sign of asking him, his ears turn forward, and I can feel his whole body settle into the gait with hardly any aides. Well, Swiss Kiss is only a fraction of the horse that Imperator is, but he does have the same way of moving when he slow-gaits. It's fun to pretend Swiss Kiss has an extra twelve inches of leg motion like Imperator. Swiss Kiss and I are always in the top two ribbons, making this season incredible. This year, Chablis Premier is the pony to beat, and the past couple shows have been challenging, trying to stay on top of our winning streak. We go into the qualifying classes casual, like a warm-up class, then we go into the championship with everything we have to give and have been almost undefeated. Even though my performance classes make my arm hairs stand straight up just thinking about them—oooh, the goosebumps—my heart feels ripped in two with the thought of what is happening in equitation.

What is happening in equitation? I don't know. I am winning my age groups, and Shammy and I have our patterns down flat. She is incredibly reliable and makes performing patterns fun. She performs on the rail like a three-gaited horse, but something seems to be falling apart. The equitation judges seem to make sure we are sometimes not even in the ribbons, dismissing us all together, while in other shows, I win everything. It's either all or nothing. I've never seen Mrs. Crabtree so upset.

Mrs. Crabtree talks about judging quite a bit because she loves to judge horse shows. Her stories were interesting and sometimes hilarious. Once, she said that she finds horses for her riders at the shows she judges, and that was a bonus, but she said she takes great pride in judging and leaves all the "politics and friendships" outside the show ring. I'm so curious about everything, so I asked her simple questions and the harder questions about judging. She told me that she doesn't ever ask for the program with names when she is judging a show. She doesn't want to know who they are or who their trainer might be, though it doesn't take long to know what horse belongs to what trainer. She just loves judging the show without all the politics, so it's about the horses and riders. Not how the horse did at the last show or at Louisville. She was excited to see them compete in front of her. One of the things she told me she did when she arrives at a show is that she asks for the time sheet and a schedule of the classes so she can have the rule book ready. I have a lot to learn. I've never read the rule book, and she helped write the rule book. One day, I can see myself judging horse shows, at least the equitation classes.

Shammy and I were heading into the arena for our class at Rock Creek Horse Show in the equitation eleven through thirteen age division. She was looking like a walk-trot champion, lacking a little of the long neck and high head that the younger and newer horses have, but her motion was incredibly high. Mrs. Crabtree said to go in and ride like it was a three-gaited stakes class, and I did! She instructed me to line up around the third horse from the end, not on the end. As always, I did exactly what she instructed me to do. I lined up third from the end, leaving about twelve riders on my right side. The judge started to walk the line from my left, inspecting each side of the rider and taking her time. That probably meant she was hitting the stirrups out from under their feet, so I was prepared and gripped hard with my legs. If she struck my stirrup, it would fall off, but my leg would remain in its exact position. I prepared for anything in my equitation classes, always thinking and always being prepared. The judge was writing on her card as she approached me, looked up from the card, and walked right past me. So confused, I couldn't imagine why she walked past me. Mrs. Crabtree let out a huff and told me to drop my reins. I was so confused that I didn't drop my reins and asked her if I should trot down to the other end and get judged there. She said, "No!"

The judge refused to judge me? Why? I'm thirteen years old. I didn't know what to do. I sat and watched Mrs. Crabtree, my heart breaking to see her so upset, so mad. This I will never forget—today's class, the judge— for the rest of my life. Are people always this mean?

Shammy and I walked back to the stalls, and I slid off her back and let Tinsley lead her into her stall. I followed and wrapped my arms around her neck. Tinsley didn't make me leave this time. Although I didn't want anyone to think I was not a good sport, I cried on Shammy's sweaty shoulder. She folded her head inward around me, her chin resting on my back, and we hugged until I stopped crying. I'm so confused. What just happened? Not only am I confused, but my heart is completely broken. Mrs. Crabtree sat me down and told me that it might be time I look for another trainer because the trainers who are judging these horse shows no longer wanted to see her riders win equitation classes. She said it was best that she retire. I don't want to find a new trainer and don't want to ride for anyone else!

My only goal for equitation for the remainder of this year was to finally win the UPHA Jr Challenge Cup, and we did, and then Shammy came home with me because she didn't belong anywhere else. She deserved to be retired, and so did Swiss Kiss. Swiss Kiss and I won almost every class this year, but the heart breaker was that we didn't win the world's championship, though as DJ said, "You gave them hell." We took home the Reserve World's Championship Five-Gaited 17 & Under title, and I was so very proud of Swiss Kiss for working so hard! As Swiss Kiss and I exited the arena, Casey Crabtree met me at the gate, and the world went black. I woke surrounded by paramedics and an IV in my arm. I guess three classes—almost in a row—at Louisville ended up taking its toll on me. I'm thankful Casey caught me before hitting the dirt.

After winning the third consecutive Three-Gaited World's Championship Pony class, Chablis Premier was sold. I don't regret that because he had several years of showing left in him and was so much fun to ride. Anyone would be lucky to have him. For a second, I was retired with Mrs. Crabtree. All I could hope for was that trainers would remember me and ask me to catch ride horses for them at horse shows if they needed someone to fill in for a rider or were trying to sell a horse. All of this work and I was done, but after Chablis Premier was sold, Mr. Redd Crabtree, the son of Mr. and Mrs. Charles Crabtree, found a three-gaited horse for me and was going to be my trainer. I shed tears of joy along with tears of sorrow, happy and sad all at the same time. I was so excited, but I also realized change was going to be difficult. I'd always imagined riding with Mr. Redd Crabtree because that's what all the other Crabtree juvenile riders seem to do, but not until after their juvenile career and when they started showing in the amateur division.

The big sorrel gelding was led out into Redd Crabtree's dark barn aisle. His name was Spencer County. He was almost as red as Liza all those years ago, and he also had a white star in the middle of his forehead. Mr. Crabtree got on him and rode him up and down the aisle a couple times before letting me get on him. He made Spencer County look like a pony with his long legs dangling down to the horse's knees. To me, Spencer County was the perfect size, powerful and bold, and I couldn't wait to see what we could accomplish together. In the back of my mind, I wish I could ride him in the equitation age division and then the three-gaited juvenile classes, but that's not how it works, nor was Mr. Crabtree an equitation instructor. Mrs. Crabtree is now battling cancer in her eye and finding it harder and harder to see. My world seems tangled.

# CHAPTER 29

## JOURNAL ENTRY: IT MUST BE A DREAM

TINSLEY TOLD ME THAT THE grooms all had a bet that if they could find a bull, I would get on and try to ride it if the bull was saddled.

"Who took the bet?" I asked.

Tinsley replied, "All agreed you'd ride the bull, so there wasn't any bet."

On occasion, other horse trainers would ask if I could ride horses for them or for their customers at shows if I wasn't riding my own. Before the World's Championship Horse Show, one of the top trainers in the country, Mr. Don Harris, asked if I could ride a five gaited pony for him at Louisville. I was so excited. I hadn't ridden a five-gaited pony since Hercules. This pony was a three-year-old gelding, a beautiful bay, who was fast as a whip, hot as a fire-cracker, and ready to go! It was more than an honor to be asked to ride, especially by a trainer like Don Harris. This pony taught me a thing or two during the class. He was like riding a lit stick of dynamite, but we survived. Mr. Harris excused us from the class at the lineup, and

I wasn't sure if I did anything wrong. He smiled and thanked me for riding this pony in his first show ever, and he didn't need to see what ribbon he would have received. This is hard for me to understand, but I did as he told me, and we left the arena. I hope I accomplished what Mr. Harris wanted me to in hopes that one day, he will ask me to ride for him again.

The year following the sale of Chablis Premier, Mr. Harris had a young three-gaited pony named Hollywood Smile, and I was honored when he asked me to ride her at Louisville. His rider had decided not to show her three-gaited pony, and they needed a catch rider. He asked if I would ride Hollywood Smile in the championship class if the rider wasn't up for the ride. In my mind, only a crazy person would say no, but I didn't know the whole story, and I knew it wasn't any of my business. I was ready and willing, but I also hoped the girl would be able to ride her pony because that would have been heartbreaking to me. All dressed but not sure if I was the rider or not, the owner decided not to ride, so Mr. Harris tossed me on, and away I went into the championship. About forty minutes later, I was in the lineup—the same class that I had won three years in a row with Chablis Premier. I felt great about this ride, but I had no idea what this pony looked like underneath me or how the other ponies compared. As we were asked to retire to the far end of the arena for the awards, I looked around at the other ponies and noticed Chablis Premier. I smiled and wondered if I was riding him, would I have won this class once more? I would never know. As I sat with the other riders and their ponies at the end of the arena, I patted this mare on the neck and told her she was a good girl. It was one of the most amazing honors as a rider to be asked to show in the world's championship class for someone else. The announcer introduced the class sponsors and the presenters into the arena. With his booming announcer voice, he said, "And your winner is…" That's my number! I saw Mr. Harris run into the arena. I was completely in shock as the announcer continued, "Hollywood Smile is your Three-Gaited World's Champion Pony."

The following year, I wasn't only showing Hollywood Smile again, but we were showing against the cutest pair at Louisville! In the arena was a cute—no, an adorable—little rider on a beautiful black three-gaited pony who stole the hearts of every person watching the show inside Louisville's Freedom Hall arena. It was actually the first time I felt big, and it was so strange to be five-foot-two and feel big. As we made our way around the arena, the crowd clapped and cheered. I needed to spot what horse was getting this attention because Hollywood Smile was becoming more afraid. She felt as if she were trying to jump out of her skin the louder the cheering levels soared. After the announcer asked for us to come in and line up for judging, they walked the line, judging the pony's confirmation. I watched as the three judges huddled together, not turning their judging cards in to the announcer. Oh boy! This means only one thing—a workout. The little girl on her beautiful black pony and myself, with Hollywood Smile, were asked to take the rail one more time at the trot. They needed to see us work again to determine who should win.

The crowd had chosen the cute little favorite! When

that tiny girl on her black steed trotted down the rail, the crowd went wild. So wild, it was ear-deafening, glass-shattering loud. It was rock-concert loud. Poor Hollywood Smile was scared to death. I headed her to the corner at the end of the arena when the loud eruption started and was trying to talk to her, to keep her mind on me instead of the sudden explosion of noise. While at the end of the arena, I simply tried to keep her in at least a jog, but I settled for a prance-walk. Anything to keep her from breaking into a canter or flying straight up into the air, which she felt as if she was going to do any moment. When the roar of the crowd started to fade, I took the straightaway at a trot, then continued a couple times around, going both ways of the arena. We lined up and waited for the results. The nice thing was that at least when the announcer called out my number as the champion, the crowd didn't boo us. Tears began to run from my eyes, goosebumps ran the inside of my riding suit, and there were no words I could say that would describe that moment in time. For me, it was five years in a row. What a dream catch ride!

I looked for my parents in the seats but couldn't find them. The world was spinning fast as Mr. Harris helped pose us for our victory picture, but as the reserve world's champion was called, the crowd ignited again with a roar of clapping and cheering that bounced from the walls and ceiling and shook the ground we stood on. It was hard to win a class where everyone in the crowd loved that little pair, but I could almost hear Mrs. Crabtree in my ear, saying, "You outrode and outsmarted them. It wasn't their year. They are young and have plenty of years ahead to win."

I have won five consecutive World's Champion Three-Gaited Pony titles prior to my seventeenth birthday. Pinch me! It truly must be a dream.

Thank goodness these catch rides weren't bulls, but the grooms are right—if it's saddled, I'll ride it. No hour of my life is wasted when I'm in a saddle, and what rides I've had! I can't believe how lucky I've been to be asked to catch ride such amazing horses and ponies. Some other important catch rides earning world's championship titles were Buck the Tiger (WC 1985), The Odalisque (WC), and a couple others—I might have forgotten their names—but I will never forget the thrill of being asked to ride and the rides we had!

*Mare and Foal*
*Sketch by Helen K. Crabtree, 1939*

# CHAPTER 30



M RS. CRABTREE DECIDED TO RETIRE, and I decided to retire with her, stepping out of the equitation division at fourteen years old. Crazy right? A simply crazy thing to do, but I made up my mind after winning the UPHA Junior Challenge Cup Championship at the American Royal Horse Show. Mrs. Crabtree begged me to go find another instructor, one that could see well; that could make me a world's champion equitation stakes rider like she thought I deserved to become. Her sight is going because of cancer.

Cancer took my grandmother, and I am having a hard time. I can't imagine what she must be going through. She is more to me than a trainer. She is my hero and my mentor. My regrets haunt me. Maybe I should have bought a new equitation horse or insisted on Spencer County, a horse more suited for equitation. Mrs. Crabtree could instruct me to be the trainer, talk me through everything, but I have no idea of what she is going through dealing with cancer and losing her one eye. I know how to read a horse, but a human…not so much.

What do I do?

Mrs. Crabtree asked if she could use a picture of me riding Spencer County on the cover of her book, the revised edition of *Saddle Seat Equitation.* It was my honor to be on the cover of her book. She signed several copies for me, and I will treasure them forever! She shared with me something she overheard someone say about me a couple years ago. They said, "This horse must be easy if this little kid can ride it." In response, she'd said, "What they don't know about this little kid is that this kid can ride."

# CHAPTER 31



## JOURNAL ENTRY: ALWAYS IN MY HEART, I WILL NEVER FORGET

SOMETHING I DIDN'T JOURNAL ABOUT, but it was really cool and I didn't want to leave it out, was the fact that I rode Chablis Premier in the Presidential Inaugural Parade for President Ronald Reagan in 1980. Mrs. Crabtree was asked if she would bring several riders and horses. We practiced and were even in the local newspaper. We dressed super warm for what was typically a cold, blizzard-like event. All bundled up, it ended up being the warmest inaugural parade ever in history and the longest, since President Reagan was busy releasing US hostages before the parade could start. Chablis Premier was quite the handful, but the opportunities Mrs. Crabtree gave me in those short few years I rode with her are priceless. Mrs. Crabtree also flew six riders and horses to France to be featured in the Paris International Equestrian Festival, the largest horse show in Europe, which was an introduction of the American Saddlebreds to Europe.

However, there are no regrets with who I became. As Mrs. Crabtree would say, I earned my Phi Beta Kappa on horseback and at the barn. These lessons proved to be priceless when used in life, so how can anyone regret that? Is your glass half empty or half full? I am simply grateful for the glass.

My favorite quote from Mrs. Crabtree is, "We must earn a horse's trust. Until that rewarding moment when the rider's understanding and the horse's trust blend, the rider will be *taking* a ride, not *making* a ride."

Her favorite saying was: "As Plutarch taught, a child's mind is not a vessel to be filled but a fire to be kindled. We may create a feeble flame or a glorious blaze, but until we dare to try, who knows?" Helen K. Crabtree, 1982

Mr. Redd Crabtree was an amazing trainer like his parents. He also won multiple world's championships. He had the best of the best horses and amateur riders riding at his barn. I had continued success in the show ring, riding Spencer County for two winning show seasons. We earned the "WC"—world's champion—to his name, winning the 17 & Under Minton Memorial 3-Gaited World's Championship trophy in 1983 and 1984. Redd had such faith in me, he entered me in the four-year-old three-gaited classes in 1986, riding MVP against all trainers, and we placed in the top five in all three shows entered, but after the sale of MVP, I disappeared from the horse world into another life adventure.

All these years later, I feel the hardest person to forgive is myself, and I still feel guilty. Maybe we should have purchased another equitation horse. Maybe I should have stayed with her and insisted she keep helping me, but I didn't. I can't go back in time. I can only treasure the time I did have with the Crabtrees at Crabtree Farms.

A few years before Mrs. Crabtree passed, she said to me, "I've trained you to be the best rider. Now maybe you can go write." I had no idea what she meant by that, but it lingered in my head. Maybe, just maybe, sharing my story of being the last Crabtree Girl is what she meant. But why would I share my personal journals with the world?

I hope you find your Liza, Vicky, Dollie, or Shammy and remember to always, always blaze your own trail and have fun! Go forward in life with no regrets and trust in yourself.

***

Dear Reader,

I hope you enjoyed reading *The Last Crabtree Girl*.

As a young girl, I was given the greatest gift of all—horses and ponies. Is there something in your life—like a pet, a hobby, a sport—that one day you will see as a life gift that helped blaze your trail?

I would love to hear your story and your thoughts about *The Last Crabtree Girl*.

Please return to your favorite online retailer to write a review.

# ACKNOWLEDGEMENTS

To my brother, Darryl, who always encouraged me to go "kick some butt."

To my husband, Todd, and my three boys, Cody, Brody, and Zane, who have had to hear my horse stories and look at all my horse photographs, trophies, and paintings their whole lives. Even though they didn't "catch the horse bug," they would go to the barn day or night to feed my horses when I was working late or traveling.

And to my friends, especially Lesley, who understood my love and devotion to my horses and put up with me for always putting my horses first!

To Anne T. Speck, Del Mar, California, my first American Saddlebred horse trainer who meant more to me than I ever expressed. Thanks for teaching me to ride American Saddle Horses, encouraging me, and training my horses, ponies, and me. Your kindness, patience, and your smile will always be in my heart.

To my dearest friend, Victoria Gillenwater, for being not only my best friend at Crabtree's but the sweetest and funniest person around! Thank you for allowing me to use the name Paula for your name in remembrance of your dad.

To my favorite groom, Red Tinsley, and his wife, Kitty.

Tina Armstrong for setting such a wonderful example in and outside of the arena when I was just a little peanut.

To Casey and Sabra Crabtree for giving me special permission to use Helen's beautiful horse sketches that are used in this book.

A special thank you to the American Saddlebred Museum, Lexington, Kentucky

# ABOUT THE AUTHOR

RA Anderson is a wanderer who has lived all over, from California to Belize, and currently, home is a town called Rome—in Georgia, that is! She grew up on horseback and sailboats, "the most amazing way to grow up!"

A lifelong passion for creative writing and photography became her life. Her award-winning photographs have been featured in table books, magazines, and front-page news, and her writing has been published in magazines, poetry books, young adult books and children's books.

Three boys—her heart and soul—call her Mom. She and her husband—"my strength and passion"—are recent empty-nesters, leaving them more time to travel.

"My life is full, colorful, and exhausting, and I wouldn't trade it for anything. However, people seem to think my most impressive accomplishment is that I know how to work the manual settings on a DSLR camera!"

**https://ra-anderson.com/**
**https://www.facebook.com/raAndersonAuthor**

# BOOKS BY RA ANDERSON

*If Pets Could Talk: Dogs*

*If Pets Could Talk: A Service Dog*

*If Pets Could Talk: Cats*

*If Pets Could Talk: Farm Animals*

*Girl Sailing Aboard the Western Star*

*Puffins Take Flight (Iceland: The Puffin Explorers Book 1)*

*Puffins Off the Beaten Path (Iceland: The Puffin Explorers Book 2)*

*Puffins Encounter Fire and Ice (Iceland: The Puffin Explorers Series Book 3)*

*Iceland: The Puffin Explorers Book of Fun Facts*